MR BYCULLA

Mr BYCULLA

A Story

By
ERIC LINKLATER

London
RUPERT HART-DAVIS
1950

To
Doyne Bell
who condoned the sacrifice

Printed in Great Britain by Richard Clay and Company, Ltd.,
Bungay, Suffolk

CHAPTER ONE

"I THINK we must admit," said Dr Lessing, with a pinched precision in his voice, "the possibility of intra-uterine memories. Like the body, mind develops gradually. There is no moment at which one can say: *Now* there is consciousness. Cognition itself has an embryonic phase in which, it is not unreasonable to suppose, an immature, uncritical sensitivity—an emergent sensitivity—may receive certain impressions that remain, like the graves of our prehistoric ancestors, to invite our speculation; to irritate, it may be, our adult craving for an explanation, for knowledge; perhaps, indeed, to haunt and perplex us with the gloom of a mystery that can never fully be resolved."

Stretched upon the sofa, Mr Byculla raised a hand whose fingers were made conspicuous, were almost disfigured, by curiously large flat nails, opaque, and yellowish in hue; and covered a noisy yawn. The left-hand corner of Dr Lessing's mouth was momentarily contorted: a spasm twice depressed his lips in a minute, half-comical grimace, and for a phrase or two after the interruption his speech was perceptibly slower than it had been. But his enunciation was still clear. He had long ago been cured of the stammer that, in his youth, had caused him such

5

convulsive misery; and all that remained of his affliction, like the scar of an old wound, was the occasional fierce twitching of his lips when he had to master some unexpected annoyance or embarrassment.

"Quite often," he continued, "I have detected, or so I believe, a definite proportion—an inverse proportion—between the actual memory and the efforts of the adult mind to re-create it in a dream. The more primitive and unspecified the initial impression, the more detailed and elaborate is our fictitious recollection of it. An over-elaborate, an excessively detailed recollection does in my opinion indicate that some of the components of the dream, if not all, are of very early origin. Even of foetal origin. Now the growing embryo must receive, and may retain in what it is perhaps permissible to call its cellular consciousness, a series of restrictive sensations. Sensations of confinement, of pressure and restraint. And volition first declares itself, it is not extravagant to assert, in tentative and fumbling movements to escape from what has become an oppressive custody."

"My mother," said Mr Byculla, "was a very big woman."

"I doubt," said Dr Lessing, a little worried, "if the actual size of the parent is of much significance. It is rather the relationship of the embryo and its maternal host——"

"But she was enormous!" declared Mr Byculla, with a leaping rhythm in his voice like the intonation of a Welshman, or an English-speaking Indian; and like the latter he sometimes used words in a way that made them bubble, as it seemed, out of the ordinary conventions of speech, like little explosions from the idiom of everyday usage. ''Yes, she was so big, like a wine-barrel, that quite often I thought she must be hollow. It was impossible to believe— but I was only a boy, of course—that she would have had strength to move about, had she been full. And what made it highly probable that she was almost, if not altogether void, were the little noises you could hear in her. Sometimes gurgle! Sometimes splash!—as if you were dropping pebble-stones into an almost-empty water-butt. I have heard echoes, going on and on, of milk-cans being trundled along the platform of a deserted railway-station. They were quite astonishing noises, I do assure you. But she was always very well dressed, in her old-fashioned way. She used to wear black satin, for choice. And she had a small black moustache that I much disliked.''

Mr Byculla himself was large, though not corpulent. The sofa on which he lay was too short for him, and hardly broad enough; but he appeared to be comfortable, and his expression was that of a man thoroughly at home in his surroundings.—He wore a grey suit, with a white stripe in it, that had been well cut by a good tailor; and his shoes were expensive. His hair grew thickly, a deep thatch of a dull copper hue with brassy gleams where it had been brushed hard and dressed with a barber's oil that smelt faintly of narcissus. A delicate nose might also have caught from his breath an odour, no stronger, of some alcoholic sweetness.

Dr Lessing's mouth was twitching again, but his thin voice betrayed no emotion when, after writing a few lines and referring to the notes he had previously made, he enquired of his patient, "You were fifteen when your mother died?"

"Fifteen and one month," said Mr Byculla. "My father and I were quite unnerved by her death, and my father, who took everything to heart, fell into a state of depression from which he might never have recovered but for a most fortunate attack of jaundice.—Jaundice, as doubtless you know, is succeeded in convalescence by extremely bad temper, which mercifully acted as counter-irritant, and no sooner was he better than he married a well-off Roumanian lady of good family.—We were, at that time, living in Salonika.—I, on the other hand, suffered only for three days, during which I cried hysterically; and immediately after the funeral, which was a grotesque ceremony, I felt such lightness of heart as I had never known before."

"I think," said Dr Lessing, "that I would prefer to leave consideration of your older years until we have explored, as well as we can, your earliest memories. Adolescence is extremely important, of course, and I have no intention of neglecting it. But let us have first things first, and discuss your dream again. The elaboration, the intricacy, of the imagined scene are very interesting; and if there is anything in my theory of an inverse proportion between the simplicity of the cause and the complexity of the effect, it must be related to some impression or occurrence of your earliest life. Now the notes I took, last Tuesday, are fairly full, and I hope accurate; but in case I omitted anything, or you forgot anything, I should like you to repeat your description of this recurrent dream——''

''Occasional,'' said Mr Byculla. ''It is not now recurrent.''

Dr Lessing referred to the neatly written pages in front of him, and said: ''It was recurrent between the ages of approximately seven years and fifteen. Since your mother died, twenty-three years ago, you have dreamed of the same scene, as far as you can remember, only three times; the last time being ten days ago.—Yes, we can now, I think, very fairly describe it as occasional rather than recurrent. But it has always begun in the same way, in the same setting of a mill or a factory?''

''I am climbing a ladder,'' said Mr Byculla, ''that leads to a trap-door in an upper storey of some tall building that is furnished with heavy, old-fashioned machinery. There is a huge iron wheel, with its outer rim most brightly polished, but I cannot see how it is supported or what purpose it serves. There are pulleys, and driving-belts that hang slack and listless, and there are cobwebs dependent from a ceiling that is partly open to let a spiral staircase reach up to some higher department, where there is more machinery. The floor on which I stand is

9

solidly made, but some of the boards are worm-
eaten, and there are small pieces of metal and bits of
rope lying about. I look round most anxiously—
but I cannot see where to hide.

"There are some people on the floor below, whis-
pering to each other. They move very quietly, but I
know they are there; and they frighten me. I control myself, however, and do not fall into panic. I
look for some place to hide, with ever-growing ur-
gency—for time is getting short—and then, without
intending such a thing, I touch a lever and start the
machinery. I am nearly caught by a driving-belt
that suddenly starts to go round, whirring and slap-
ping, and above the mechanical noise I hear the
angry shouting of those who are below.

"Now my mood changes. I do not want to hide,
I want to escape. I must escape! And just when I
am near to desperation, I see what I had not seen before: a little door."

"Do you remember," asked Dr Lessing, "what
sort of door it was?"

"It was quite narrow," said Mr Byculla promptly,
"under a pointed arch in the best fashion of English
Perpendicular. There were two small but fanciful
iron hinges on the door, and the spandrel above was
decorated with a nice quatrefoil design."

"Did you observe all that, and identify the design, at the age of seven?"

"The dream was recurrent until I was fifteen, by
which time I was certainly familiar with all common
types of architecture. My parents, though undesir-

able in many ways, had highly artistic interests, and my father, who collected Russian ikons, had also a Picasso of the Blue period.''

''Yes, yes,'' said Dr Lessing. ''You must forgive me. Not all my patients have so broad a background.—Please continue. You opened the door, and what did you see?''

''A short corridor with cream-coloured walls on which, in gilt frames, were water-colour paintings of tropical flowers. This corridor led into a smallish room furnished with an Empire sofa and three or four chairs well upholstered in blue-and-white striped satin. There was then a long chain of rooms, one opening into another, and some of the doorways and the decoration were Moorish or Arabian. Room followed room quite like the stories in the Arabian Nights, but some were incongruously decorated and most disconcerting. In one there was a fountain playing in a marble basin, and in the next—you have been in the Vatican, perhaps?''

''No,'' said Dr Lessing.

''In the Vatican,'' said Mr Byculla, ''there are reception rooms that are furnished after somewhat austere pattern. At one end there is a Throne, at the other a Crucifix. I found myself in a room like that, standing on a very cold mosaic floor, and my fear became panic. I began to whimper! Those who were pursuing were coming closer, I could hear them shutting doors behind them, and on ahead there were others waiting. I could not yet see them, but I knew what they were like. They had long

11

legs, and their heads—you know what *ooplah* means?''

''I'm afraid not.''

''It is Indian word for large patty-cakes of cowdung, used for making fire.—So then, quite in despair, I turn away from the *ooplah*-men, and on my right I find another door, and more beyond it. But now the air is bad, there is not much light, and behind the doors there are people sleeping.

''In one room—I know it by his smell—there is an old man, as old as the hills, who is about to die. In another, a fat fishmonger and his snoring wife. In a third, two maiden ladies, lean and angry, breathing hoarsely. In a fourth, a girl with eyes like a pig, she is soft and too large.—I am terrified of waking them, and I come out, tip-toe, on a little landing from which small, white-painted banisters lead downstairs. Here I am more happy, for the stairs lead down to a warm, well-lighted room where I shall be quite safe.—But now it is too late! On all sides I hear doors opening, as if they were hungry, as if they were drawing in their breath, and I know that my pursuers have found me. The *ooplah*-men are behind me, the sleepers have come out of their beds—and calling to my mother, I fall in dead faint!''

''The sensation of fainting was quite definite, was it?'' asked Dr Lessing.

''It was, I thought, the sensation of death,'' said Mr Byculla. ''When I woke up I could not, for a long time, believe that I was still alive.''

The air in the consulting-room had become a little

stale, and Dr Lessing got up to open a window. Mr Byculla, who in an outmoded fashion carried a handkerchief tucked into his left sleeve, above a gold wrist-watch on a bracelet of gold wire, pulled it out and wiped his cheeks and forehead. His chest, rising and falling, betrayed his quickened breathing.

Dr Lessing, sniffing once or twice, said to him, "Your physical condition is very good indeed. The laboratory reports are all perfectly satisfactory."

"I have an excellent constitution," said Mr Byculla.

"Are you a temperate man? Do you drink much?"

"No, no. Very little. Some brandy at night, perhaps, and I am fond of liqueurs.—These also are very good. Have one."

From a pocket Mr Byculla took a small paper-bag in which there remained two or three liqueur chocolates. "They are French, they are excellent," he said, and helped himself.

Dr Lessing took one, rather doubtfully, and laid it on his desk. "Perhaps later," he said, and for some time discussed with his patient his daily regimen. Then, having looked over his notes again, he asked, "You are feeling quite well and confident now, are you?"

"I am A-1," said Mr Byculla. "I am in splendid trim. When I was telling my dream, I got somewhat excited, but that has now passed. I am feeling tip-top."

"Then I'll say good-bye till next Tuesday. I don't want to tire you——"

"Nor I you," replied Mr Byculla with a courteous inclination; and rose from the sofa. He was five or six inches taller than the Doctor, and when he smiled he revealed a set of excellent large teeth. His features were bold and regular, and his good looks were marred only by a coarse and sallow skin, and eyes that were flecked with yellow or tawny streaks.

From a wallet of morocco leather, initialled in gold, he took a £5 note, twice-folded, and spreading it open on the Doctor's desk, said with another smile, "I am giving you a lucky one. You see the number?"

"0 13 575310," read Lessing. "Is that supposed to be lucky? I'll send it to Sir Simon, if it is. I owe him five pounds, and it's a long time since he's had anything like good luck."

"It is a most highly auspicious number," answered Mr Byculla, and fetched from his trouser-pocket two half-crowns. "Let us toss for the oddments," he proposed.

"Well," said Lessing, taken aback, "it's unusual, but——"

"You make your livelihood from the unusual, so you should not take exception to it," said Mr Byculla, spinning a coin towards the ceiling. "You call."

"Er, heads," said Lessing.

"Tails it is," said Mr Byculla, and pocketed the half-crowns. "Till next Tuesday, Doctor."

CHAPTER TWO

In a shabby woollen dressing-gown that concealed a pair of new satin knickers and a brassière of almost Cretan arrogance—in its cusps her small flaccid breasts challenged as proudly as the insolent womanhood of Cnossos—Claire Lessing was painting with a scarlet pencil the outermost parts of her wide but thinly drawn mouth. Grimacing first to one side, then to the other, she daubed and carefully enlarged her meagre lips, so colouring the adjacent skin as to present an appearance, at some distance or in a poor light, of physical generosity, and thereby suggest a temperament of more liberality than in fact she owned. But the general structure of her face denied the pretence of lipstick, and though she disliked the narrowness of her forehead, and sometimes dreaded the effect of age on her pointed chin, she never failed to admire the thin white aquilinity of her nose, in spite of the insistence with which it contradicted the red promise of her mouth.

She moved a wing of her three-paned looking-glass to examine her profile, and lengthened a little the drawn curve of her left eyebrow . . . With what definition, she remembered, the rakish cap of the Auxiliary Nursing Yeomanry had flattered her looks during those ever-to-be-regretted years of war when she had driven a fast car, with the speed and composure of perfect mastery, and enjoyed, with a greed that she rarely betrayed, the admiration of the innumerable officers whose duty took them, in the seat beside her or the seat behind, to Colchester and Netley, to Bath and Shrewsbury and Liverpool and York. Duty itself had brought pleasure to her life, and duty, often enough, had led or deviated towards the small exaggerations of living, those trivial excitements, in which she found the satisfaction she desired.—Dancing, with other partners waiting near the door; gin before lunch, and whisky and soda late in the evening; the wary love-making of elderly officers, and their occasional small presents; the agitated desire of young men to seduce her, and their surliness or self-pity when they failed.—She had not often yielded herself entirely, and never out of weakness except to her cousin Ronnie Killaloe; but to arouse, by progressive small submissions, the belief that she was about to yield, and then abruptly to refuse what she had seemed to promise, had given a relish to many excursions in the summer and winter evenings in cold hotels.

On a chest of drawers stood large photographs, silver framed, of herself in uniform and George Lessing unconvincingly attired as a Lieutenant-Colonel of the R.A. M.C.—She stood up to put off her dressing-gown, and pulled open a drawer without looking at them. Colonel Lessing, indeed, had never engaged her affection, but when the war came to an end, and her pleasant occupation with it, she had agreed resentfully to marry him: resentful against a world that had deprived her of a fast car and amusing passengers, perversely resentful against Lessing himself because he alone, since the recklessness of 1940, had offered marriage. She had refused him more than once, for he bored her at their first meeting, and he was so ill-suited in uniform that she was half-ashamed to be seen with him; but when peace returned, ungraciously enough, to reduce the importance of many of her most agreeable acquaintances, and obscure their gallantry in patched civilian suits, George Lessing's apparent value was enhanced and his income not diminished. His civil practice, as a psychiatrist, began to revive as soon as his prospective patients had the leisure to recognise their anxieties.

Dressed now, adorned and scented, Mrs Lessing went to the kitchen for a jug of water, and from a cabinet in the sitting-room took glasses and a bottle of gin. She drank impatiently, looking at the clock.

"Has that man been with you till now?" she asked, when Lessing, wearing a slightly complacent, slightly quizzical expression—a scholar appreciating a scholar's private joke—at last came in.

"I had to write my notes," he answered. "I've got a rare and curious bird this time—you haven't seen him, have you?—but I think I'm getting somewhere with him. Just before he left——"

"I'm sorry, George, but I can't stay and listen to you now. You're very late——"

"Are you going out?"

"Do you think I've dressed like this to stay at home with you?"

"I hadn't really noticed. I was thinking of something else.—Where are you going?"

"To dine with Ronnie. I told you on Sunday."

"But I asked you to put him off."

"Well, I thought you were quite unreasonable, and I didn't."

"I had a reason that any reasonable person would find sufficient, and if you——"

"You had nothing but selfishness and your old ridiculous jealousy. If I'd ever given you any cause for jealousy, it would be different."

"If I was jealous, it wasn't for the usual cause. I was jealous of your reputation, not of your love."

"Oh, don't be a fool, George. You speak as if this was 1914."

"Even in 1949, in this country at least, people take a fairly serious view of murder."

"But Ronnie isn't a murderer! It was proved, beyond the shadow of a doubt, that he was in Highgate at the time!"

"He had been with the girl earlier in the evening. He was a friend of hers. And in a case of murder it isn't only the murderer and his victim who suffer. All who are connected with it are sullied—and because I don't want your name to be soiled as well, I'd prefer you to break off all relations with your cousin."

"Are you being quite honest, George? Is that

18

your real reason, or is it only a convenient new disguise for your old jealousy of Ronnie?''

Lessing hesitated before he answered, and his mouth began to twitch. ''I don't think so,'' he said. ''I believe I'm being perfectly honest. The reason I gave you was a sufficient reason; and even though my opinion of your cousin may be biased, my dislike of murder is quite impersonal.''

''But Ronnie wasn't the murderer!''

''I've already explained——''

''Why don't you save time by admitting that what you want is to own me, body and soul, and have me at your beck and call from morning till night?''

''You might think more clearly, and understand things better, if you avoided *clichés*——''

''Oh, damn you, George, don't be such an old fogey! You talk about understanding, but where's yours? If I were a patient you'd have some sympathy for me, but as I'm only your wife I get nothing but lectures and complaints.—When did you last give me credit for any decent motive? Do you think Ronnie's happy at this moment? Do you think, because a man's been unlucky, that everyone ought to avoid him as if he was a leper? He's alone in the world, all alone except for his father, who takes no notice of him, takes no notice of anything except a lot of old books in the British Museum. And he is, after all, my cousin.''

Supine, as though collapsed, he lay in a deep chair and listened to her with aching ears. Her voice had grown shrill, and quite suddenly he had felt upon

19

his mind the burden of inordinate repetition, and admitted his weariness. He had listened, so often before, to this sort of argument. By the sheer persistence of her indomitably selfish will, by the mere extent of her superficiality, by the profundity of her unreason and her elastic indifference to logic, he had been defeated again and again. Always defeated.

"You used to understand me," she said. "You were the only one who ever did, and that's why I fell in love with you. That, and your generosity.—My God, how mean some of those others were! And a mean man's no good to a woman. Every woman knows that. But it's never been a fault of yours.— And there, if you really want to know, is what was at the back of my mind when I said I'd go and dine with Ronnie this evening. He's hard up, naturally, but I knew I could rely on you. You're difficult, George, God knows you're difficult, but you're not mean and never were; and when you're not feeling tired and unhappy and suspicious, you know perfectly well that you can trust me. You can trust me as you would yourself."

"I suppose you know," he said dully, "that we're overdrawn again."

"But that's only temporary. You've got a good practice, and it's getting better. All those patients coming week after week, and paying guineas every time——"

"Not all of them. There are those who pay nothing."

"But the others make up for that.—Oh, George,

don't look so old! It makes me miserable to see you like that. Let me give you another drink to cheer you up."

She took his glass, sprinkled bitters in it, filled it half-full of gin, and added water.

"How much do you want?" he asked.

"Give me five pounds. I shan't need all that, but it's wretched not to have enough; and I'll bring you the change."

He wanted only to get rid of her now, he had no more inclination for argument; and from his pocket-book he took a twice-folded £5 note.—"But no, not this," he said. "I'll give you a cleaner one. I'll keep this for old Killaloe."

"How do you come to owe him money?"

"I bought that picture from him. He was sending his collection to Sotheby's, to be sold, to raise enough to pay for your cousin's defence."

"How much was it?"

"It wasn't dear."

"And while you talk about my extravagance, you pay good money for a thing like that!"

"I like it."

"Well, everyone to his taste, but I think it's morbid."—She bent, and offered him her cheek to kiss. "Thank you, George. I shan't be late," she said, "but don't wait up for me if you're tired. I gave Clarissa a powder an hour ago—her tooth was worrying her—and I shouldn't think she'll wake before I get back. You'll be all right, won't you?"

He waited until he heard the slam of the outer

door, and then got up to look at the small picture he had bought, two days before, from Sir Simon Killaloe.

An antelope, surprised, watched from a patch of jungle, painted in a delicately exact convention, a scene of murder on a lonely road beneath a darkening sky. The antelope, enamelled blossoms, and the victim's yellow coat and bright-blue turban gave the picture, as a picture, an attractive innocence; but the dead man's gaping mouth cried piteously of mortality, and the murderers, in their hieratic intensity, were engines of assassination with gleaming eyes.— "The Kangra school, late eighteenth century," Sir Simon had explained. "There was a little renaissance of Hindu art, and the revival of Thuggee dated from about the same time."

Lessing, who had never seen Indian painting before, was deeply moved by the grave and formal charm of his picture. The two Thugs were drawn, with no hint of antipathy or caricature, in the same degree of abstraction as had found for the antelope and the bright sprays of blossom a pretty though serious convention. Only in his treatment of the man who had been strangled did the artist appear to have given way to inartistic feeling, to distaste: in the ungainliness of his attitude there was a suggestion of mockery.—"Or am I seeing too much?" Lessing murmured. "Is that subjective vision?"

An old bewilderment returned to him when he sat down again with his unfinished drink; for he was a kindly man who could not quite subdue his kindliness by regarding it as emotional instability, nor dismiss a general pity by identifying it with self-pity. After a quarrel with his wife, or ill-temper between them, he was always sorry to have upset her, and would examine his arguments to see if he had been unjust.—That he was, or had been, jealous of Ronnie Killaloe, he readily admitted; and the shabby record of Ronnie's life made his jealousy the more galling. But this matter of a murder, and Ronnie's connexion with it, was surely something that could be dissociated from personal feeling: any normal man, in comparable circumstances, would have spoken as he had. —But many women, perhaps, who certainly could not be described as abnormal, would have sided with Claire? The impulse to succour a young man, good-looking and lonely, had the force of instinct; to abstain from his company because his reputation, poor enough before, had been soiled in a court of law, was merely a social injunction of brief authority. The very fact that Ronnie now stood a little beyond the pale of respectable society, was in some sort an exile or a foreigner, was possibly a further attraction.

"Women are exogamous," said Lessing to the gin bottle, "and I quarrelled with her because she is a woman. We made the tribe, and made its laws, and we are jealous in order to keep the laws. But if the laws had always been kept—the laws of strict endogamy—the tribe would have degenerated. Women are lawless by instinct—and have I the right to blame her for what she is?"

23

From the room next door, but little muted by the wall, came the snarling cry of a small child, already habituated to complaint, demanding his attention. It grew louder, rose to an agitated howl, then stopped while the child wondered if it had been heard. . . . It began again, quietly at first, but soon reached the pitch of fury, and with intervals of a minor lament, returned to it again and again with nagging intensity.

"On the other hand," said Lessing, getting up and going to the door, "I may be flattering her. Perhaps I should describe her as half a woman."

CHAPTER THREE

CLAIRE LESSING and Ronnie Killaloe came out of a restaurant in Charlotte Street, and in the warm September dusk walked slowly westward. He had surprised her by paying for their dinner—paying without any comment on the bill, without the little grimace and half-mocking glance that had so often invited her to deal with it—and now, after they had walked for half a mile or so, she contentedly enough, holding his arm and leaning against him a little, he astonished her again by calling to a passing cab and giving the driver the address of his attic-flat in Batavia Street, off Warwick Avenue.

"You haven't been as well-to-do as this for years," she said. "If you've got a job, it can't be honest."

"I don't get jobs," he answered, "nearly so often as I get good ideas. Sometimes they're my own, sometimes they're other people's. This was handed to me on a plate by one of the Sunday papers."

"What was it?"

"To write the life-story, in two thousand words, of Fanny Bruce."

"Have you done it?"

"Of course I have: they offered me fifty guineas.

It wasn't enough, I admit, but it was better than nothing.''

"It didn't strike you as being a bit caddish, to write that sort of thing?''

"She's dead, poor girl. It won't hurt her.''

"And it won't hurt you, I suppose, because you're not very sensitive?''

"I can't afford to be.''

"Some people——''

"Oh, shut up. I didn't ask you to come out and criticise me.''

"Will it be signed? With your own name?''

"'By Ronnie Killaloe. The Dead Girl's Best Friend.'''

"My God, Ronnie! What will your father think?''

"He won't see it. It's not the sort of paper that goes into his club.''

"But if he did——''

"Well, what of it? He's getting hardened to punishment, and I can't say I'm sorry.''

"You used to have some decent feelings, Ronnie——''

"Not about him. He was as proud as Lucifer of my two brothers, before they were killed, but he always looked at me as if I was something the cat had found.—And because the pride of Lucifer is rather more than we can stomach nowadays, he was punished. He was badly punished. He's only got me now. Me, and that loud-voiced intellectual that Edward married, and he can't stand her either. She's going to bring up his grandchildren without any re-spect for the past, without any reverence for the good old days that he enjoyed; and he can't forgive her that, because he can't forgive the times we live in. He's only sixty-three, but you'd think he was in the middle seventies : well, that's due to pride, and his refusal to face facts.—And talking of that, you're not getting any younger either. I do believe these gentle curves are filling out at last. Is George still good to you?''

''He trusts me, at any rate,'' she answered bitterly.

''He's the sort of psychiatrist I'll go to, when I have to. I'm all for those who've got faith in others.—Left here, driver, and stop by that lamp-post.''

She followed him up a long, awkward stair, with a loudly cracking step on the last flight, and before a cracked mirror in his bedroom repaired her maquil-lage. She heard the flushing of a water-closet, and for a minute or two waited, suddenly resenting all the dirt and shabbiness, in the small undusted sit-ting-room, under a sloping ceiling, until he ap-peared with a bottle of brandy in one hand, two bottles of ginger ale in the other, and tumblers in the pockets of his coat.

''You can call it Hennessy, or Courvoisier, or Biscuit Dubouché,'' he said. ''You can call it simple rot-gut, and still I'd like it. Late at night or at ten o'clock to-morrow morning, it's what I need to face the abomination of the sun, the plague of fortune, and the God-damned dark!—You're looking bad-tempered, Claire, and all the prettier for it. Drink that, and don't drink it like a connoisseur, drink it like a horse."

"I don't want it," she said.

"Well, that's a blow.—Why not?"

"I don't like your making money by writing articles about that girl."

"There was only one."

"Did you tell the truth in it?"

"To some extent."

"Have you ever told the truth—the whole truth—about her?"

"Of course."

"I want to know—about you and her."

"Don't you read the papers?"

"Yes, I read them. I've read them for years. And that's why I'm asking you to tell me the truth."

"I didn't murder her, if that's what you mean."

"All right, then. Tell me who did."

"I wish I knew. I was half in love with her."

"Honestly?"

"Yes."

"What was she like?"

"She was different," he said, and Claire sneered.

"Yes, I know!" he exclaimed. "It rings like a bad half-crown, doesn't it? But it happens to be true."

He lay back in a chair cushioned with a stained and faded green corduroy, a chair with a movable back that creaked and groaned as it took his weight. —He was a handsome young man, and would have

28

been handsomer with good grooming and a healthier habit of life. Lean of face, tolerably broad of shoulder, long in the thigh; his black hair grew thickly, and had not lately been cut. His cheeks were deeply lined from the flanges of his nose to the corners of his mouth, his teeth were square and white, except at one side, where decay had been neglected. His eyes were yellowish between puffy lids, and his fingers tobacco-stained. His double-breasted jacket and unpressed trousers, of dark blue faintly striped, were indistinguishable from several thousand other suits in London, and his shoes needed resoling.

"I don't want to quarrel with you," said Claire unhappily. "You know how I feel. But I've got to know. You must tell me about her. Or else——"

"What?"

"Well, I can't go back to what we were.—I don't even know how long you were friends. I don't know how you met her."

"What about a drink?"

"Yes, I think I will."

"It was in February," said Ronnie. "There was that spell of good weather, you remember, a kind of false spring, and she was wearing a grey-flannel skirt and a white jersey. She was bare-headed, and looked about seventeen. She had a dog on a lead: an Airedale, of all things. She came round the corner of Cork Street into Burlington Gardens and said, 'Wouldn't you like to make friends with me and my dog?'—Well, I knew it was a gag, of course, but she looked so damned young. She *was* young! She

29

hadn't been at the game for more than two or three months.''

''And then?''

''I went with her, and a few days later I met her again. That's where I made a mistake. I got into the habit, and she fell in love with me. I told you she was young.''

''And you were going out with her—and I was paying for you!—at the same time!''

''Well, you know how it is.—Oh, what the hell!''

''Yes, what the hell!—And what happened next?''

''She got into trouble with the people who were running her. They're organised, those girls. They're given a decent flat and smart clothes, and they turn over what they earn and get a percentage. It's little enough.—Well, she started to make trouble. She started fighting with the men she picked up, and said she couldn't go on.''

''Why not?''

''She wanted me to take her away. It was a proper case. She was in love with me, and I—well, what could I do? I hadn't any money, I never have had any. I couldn't keep myself, let alone her. But one night—that was the last night—I met her, and she said she was going to drown herself if I didn't help her. I was as worried as hell, and it just happened that I'd picked up about eleven pounds at Harringay the night before, and I gave her half of what I'd got, and some good advice. I told her to work as hard as she could for the next couple of weeks, and hold out on the people who were running her. I told her that if she could make seventy or eighty pounds I'd take her to the South of France, and between the two of us we'd try to make a living out of American tourists. We sat in a little café at the back of Bolton Street—she wouldn't go to a pub, she never drank—and argued till about half-past ten or eleven o'clock——"

"Till eleven?"

"It was getting on for that."

"But you said in court that you'd left her at nine!"

"Well, I met a fellow I'd known in Cairo, he's a journalist now, and he took me out to Highgate and gave me a drink or two. And when things began to look bad for me, he agreed to say that I'd met him about half-past nine, and spent the rest of the night with him."

"Doesn't anyone tell the truth nowadays?"

"Not many," said Ronnie. "Not among the sort of people we know."

"Speak for yourself," said Claire.

"It's about time you had another drink, isn't it?"

"I don't know. I don't think I will. I think I'll go home."

"No, not yet."

"I'm not going to stay unless you swear to me she was alive when you left her, and——"

"I don't need to swear. It's true."

"You never saw her again? And she *was* alive?"

"She was alive all right. She tucked the fiver I'd

given her into the top of her stocking, and blew her nose, and said, 'Death to the French!'—There's a lot of Belgian tarts about nowadays, who pretend they're French, and they were the ones, she said, who were taking most of the trade. But she was all out to make money, after what I'd promised her.— And then I left her.''

''At eleven o'clock?''

''A little before that.''

''And an hour later a policeman found her in that street or lane, there's only a few yards of it, off the north side of Berkeley Square——''

''Jones Street.''

''—with her neck broken.''

''She can't have suffered,'' said Ronnie. ''It must have been a quick death, whoever did it.''

''What happened to her dog? The Airedale?''

''She'd had to give it up. It used to bark, and some of her customers didn't care for that.''

''It might have saved her life. I had a fox-terrier once; it wouldn't let anyone come near me.''

''That wouldn't have got you far in her profession.''

''You oughtn't to make jokes about it. It's not right.''

''Well, let's forget about it, and have another drink. Where's your glass? It's not often I've got a bottle of brandy in the house.''

''No, I don't want any more. I'm going home.''

''Oh no, you're not. Not yet, at any rate.''

''I want to, Ronnie.''

32

"What you want's what I want, and don't pretend it isn't.—Give me your glass.—If we can't be honest all the time, and you've got to admit it's difficult in times like these, let's do the best we can, and be honest after dark. And don't let's break an old habit."

CHAPTER FOUR

"WHAT have I got to live for?" Sir Simon repeated. "Well, when you put it to me as bluntly as that, I'm bound to answer, Not much. I still enjoy a cup of good coffee when I can get it, I like the morning sensation of being newly shaved, I find it agreeable to talk about India with anyone who has the patience to listen and some small knowledge of the subject—and so on. There are many little pleasures in the world, and the sum of them, I suppose, gives me reason enough, or at least the impulse, to live from day to day. But my life, I admit, has no longer any particular aim; and perhaps not much purpose."

"You cannot be pleased to live in such a place as this," said Mr Byculla, looking at the shabby Victorian wardrobe, the faded green carpet, the wash-hand basin, the single bed under its eiderdown quilt of artificial silk.

"I've been spoiled, I suppose. I had grown accustomed to big rooms, and plenty of them. In the early part of my service I lived very simply, and often quite roughly; and thought nothing of it. I'd no time to, for one thing, and young men don't attach much importance to comfort; or they didn't in my day. But later on, of course, I lived very well, and got used to a certain spaciousness; even, perhaps, to

35

what many people to-day would regard as some degree of splendour. And the transition from that sort of life to this, from India under the British raj to a cheap hotel under our contemporary brand of Puritanism, has been rather violent.—No, I don't really enjoy living in austerity on the plains of Kensington."

"I also do not much like it," said Mr Byculla, "but I make shift to put up with it in order to enjoy certain luxuries that otherwise I could not afford. I have always been much averse to depriving myself of luxury; but comfort I can do without. And for me it is quite easy to reconcile myself to the Beauvoir Private Hotel, because, unlike you, I have no background of splendour to jeer and make mock of it."

Seated on a cane-bottomed bedroom-chair, Mr Byculla's large body looked enormous, and his balance appeared to be precarious. But whether they sat in his bedroom or Sir Simon's, he always insisted that Sir Simon take the arm-chair—one was covered in a scratched leather, the other in a flower-patterned chintz—and on his own exiguous seat betrayed no unease, by shifting and changing his position, but like a cavalry officer in his saddle sat upright for an hour at a time.

They had known each other, with a gradually increasing intimacy, for nearly a couple of months.— In the Reading Room of the British Museum, Mr Byculla, himself an occasional student, had been interested one day to see an elderly man, of the most distinguished bearing, carrying with a curious humility the poor scholar's burden of a dozen obscure, ponderous, and shabby books. Tall and silver-haired, his face unblemished ivory, he wore that look of exceeding patience which is sometimes the patrician mask of arrogance: the patience of a man who for many years has sat in judgment over others, issuing his commands, and heard a thousand tales of crime and folly, and learnt to expect little else from poor humanity. But now—for he was clearly unused to burdens of a material sort, and carried his books most clumsily—now the ruler's patience had been transmuted and brought down to the resignation of a humble student.—That ivory head, thought Mr Byculla, deeply interested by what he saw and what he guessed, may well have been the head and centre of courts and crowds, guarded by troopers on black horses; and now like a labourer he carries books of the dustiest sort, mere bricks of learning, waiting to be built . . .

Two fell, and then another, fluttering open on the floor. Mr Byculla stooped to pick them up, and with a brief murmur was thanked for his help. He looked curiously at the titles of the volumes, and an hour or so later found an opportunity to glance at the pages of a schoolboy's exercise-book in which the patrician had been writing. With more understanding than might have been expected, he read:

Thori.   *Rajput origin claimed as usual. Marwar Census Report* (1891) *inconclusive.*

Kaikadis	{ *Kamathis: men basket-makers, women prostitutes.*
	{ *Bhamtas: pickpockets.*

Affinity of Kaikadis with Kolhatis because both keep donkeys. Kolhati girls choose between marriage and acrobatics + prostitution.

Worship Mahadev and the wrestler Maruti— but their living gods are "the drum, the rope, and the balancing pole".

Mangs.   *Sarnaiks the leaders in crime.*

Widows re-marry by night at dark of the moon. Sorcerers, rope-makers, and hangmen. (Post hoc ergo propter hoc?)

All hereditary robbers except Dakalvars.

Sopachas (?)—dog-feeders—are minstrels and poets to the Mangs . . .

"You are interested?" asked the patrician, returning quietly to his seat.

"Most humbly I beg your pardon," said Mr Byculla, taken by surprise and much embarrassed. "Yes, I am interested, but that is no excuse——"

"It is, however, almost a compliment.—No, there is no need to apologise."

Mr Byculla, however, waited for half an hour until the patrician, having finished his studies for the day, got up to go; and following him, insisted on expressing the extremest penitence for his rudeness. He too, he explained, was deeply interested in India, especially in the lowest castes and least fortunate of its people.

"My maternal great-grandmother," he said, "was

38

a *devadasi*, a temple prostitute, from Trichinopoly. My great-grandfather, a clerk in the East India Company, abducted her——"

"Have you proof of that?"

"I can show you family papers," said Mr Byculla, bending forward a little in his anxiety and eagerness —his great arms extended, his copper-coloured head thrust forward, so that he looked, on the steps of the British Museum, like a huge animated statue of supplication.—"I have a great deal of information about my forebears, who on both sides had Indian connexion."

"Well," said the other, a little doubtfully, "I shall be in the Reading Room again to-morrow."

"That is most kind of you," said Mr Byculla. "I also shall be here, and you will be highly interested, I promise you, in my ancestral documents.—May I enquire your name, please?"

"Killaloe . . ."

Ten days later Mr Byculla took a room in the Beauvoir Private Hotel, where Sir Simon Killaloe, K.C.S.I., C.I.E., had for some months been living in a dreary loneliness that was more than physical.— The Empire he had served was no more, and none but a grey-haired minority seemed to regret its passing. Without emotion, without turning their heads to see it go, the English had shrugged off their vast dominion in utter indifference not merely to their own achievements there, but to the consequences of what they had done, and did not do. Sir Simon, who knew the vanity of bitterness, knew also the relativity of age: he was old beyond his years because he was the survivor of an age that had gone. And survivors, like castaways, live on desolate shores.— He had even survived those of his own name, for his wife had died long ago, and the war had left his two elder sons at Keren and in the sea off Matapan. Only the youngest, the wastrel, was left, like an open seam that could not be caulked, and two small grand-children, both of them girls, whose mother was too confidently modern—too shallow, it might be, for him to find any solace in her company. His un-likely friendship with Mr Byculla had given him more pleasure than, as he had sometimes thought, there still remained in life.

The pedigree, in which Mr Byculla took ingenu-ous pride, had been his first delight. The great-grandmother who was a *devadasi* in Trichinopoly—there was good evidence as to her profession—had borne and nurtured, with the help of a runaway clerk of the East India Company, a young man called Devereux, an engine-driver on the Great In-dian Peninsula Railway, who, marrying the Irish widow of a sergeant in the Highland Light Infantry, had prospered uncommonly by reason, it appeared, of some talent for usury; and left the railway to be-come an indigo-planter in Bengal. His daughter, an only child and convent-educated, was Mr Byculla's mother.

There was the distaff-side, and on the spear-side loomed in the distance a Marwari merchant from Jaisalmer, who in pursuit of fortune had gone to

Singapore, and there lived for some time with an Armenian carpet-seller's daughter; who, when he deserted her, had kept a lodging-house and subsequently a small restaurant. Their child—hers and the Marwari's—grew to exceptional beauty, and won the heart of a Mr McKillop, a marine engineer from Govan, on the Clyde. Seven young McKillops, all of them energetic and acquisitive, were presently scattered over half the world, from Alexandria to Manila, of whom one, Mr Byculla's father, settled in Beirut, where he made a considerable fortune as—said Mr Byculla—an importer. On business in Calcutta he met and wooed the indigo-planter's daughter; and of their union Mr Byculla, his two sisters having died in infancy, was the sole remaining issue.

"So your name," Sir Simon had remarked, after studying these unusual antecedents, "is really McKillop? Why do you call yourself Byculla?"

"To remind myself, every day, of the vanity of human wishes.—But that, as explanation, is what you call cryptic, is it not? You must let me unravel it by telling you of my poor lamented father's great ambition.—He was a most ambitious man, and highly individual. A good business man, and deeply religious from time to time. He would join every religion in turn, to see what it was about, and that greatly annoyed my mother, who was a staunch Catholic. But my father was also a snob, and when he went to Bombay to extend his business, he set his heart on becoming a member of that most exclusive and superior clique, the Byculla Club; and did what he could to make himself acceptable. He gave away large sums to charity, to hospitals, to the Governor's Fund when there was a famine, and so on and such like. Then he wrote to the Secretary of the Club, and promised that if he were made a member he would have constructed for it, at his own expense, an up-to-date, brand-new swimming-pool.''

''Poor man,'' said Sir Simon. ''Did he get a reply?''

''From the Secretary,'' said Mr Byculla, ''there came nothing but impermeable silence. From other mouths, however, when my father complained of such treatment, there issued heartless laughter, and my father, wounded to the core, bitterly regretted the money he had wasted on hospitals and the Governor's Fund for a famine. He never forgot the injury he had received, and died a much-disappointed man.—But that was in Beirut, of course. We did not live very long in Bombay.''

''It's a sad story,'' Sir Simon observed, ''and you must have shared your father's disappointment before you decided to commemorate it.''

''Oh no,'' said Mr Byculla, ''not at all. It was during the war that I found it advisable to adopt another name, while I was engaged upon certain delicate operations.''

''What were you doing?''

''I was a secret agent. Not well paid, but highly trusted and very successful.—I had many advantages, of course, having lived in Beirut when I was young.

In Beirut a boy can be much better educated than in England, where he does not grow up until it is too late.—I spoke several languages, and had had much experience. So at first I went to Ankara, then to Constanza, to Bucharest; to small places like Dedeagatch and Pleven, and once as far as Graz.—But before I went anywhere at all I decided to call myself *Mr Byculla* and remind myself every day that I must not repeat my father's mistake and become too ambitious. To be ambitious when you are also a secret agent is highly imprudent.''

Sir Simon, in his loneliness, found Mr Byculla an engaging companion—he begged for a copy of the exotic family tree—and their casual acquaintanceship ripened surprisingly into friendship when he discovered that Mr Byculla had a considerable, though unsystematic, knowledge of the criminal tribes of India. The study of these proscribed, yet tolerated, castes and classes was almost the sole occupation of Sir Simon's leisure, and he still hoped to finish the book he had long been writing and prove that in the beginning they had constituted an integral and necessary part of Hindu society. To discuss, then, with Mr Byculla the marriage rites, for example, of the Lamani—some of whom are professional thieves—and identify so much of the ceremony with pure Brahminical practice, gave him the liveliest pleasure; and very soon after Mr Byculla came to live at the Beauvoir Private Hotel, they formed the habit of retiring after dinner to one or the other's bedroom, to make their own coffee and drink a glass or two of brandy. Sir Simon had a small wooden case, made like a miniature trunk of some dark wood inlaid with brass, that held three decanters and six little crystal goblets: sea-captains in the eighteenth century often carried such a useful receptacle. And Mr Byculla, greatly admiring it, searched antique-shops until he found another of the same sort, and could entertain Sir Simon on his own terms.

It was Sir Simon who had advised him to consult Dr Lessing when he complained of bad dreams.—"I know nothing about psychiatrists myself," he said, "but everybody seems to go to them nowadays, and I don't suppose they can do a fellow much harm so long as he keeps his head and doesn't believe all they tell him.—I met George Lessing when he married a cousin of my wife's, and I see him from time to time. I took quite a liking to him.—I think he worries too much, but so should I, I expect, if I'd married a girl like that. I don't suppose he's got much judgment, but he's certainly clever, and I should say he's honest.—Anyway, psychiatrists are the only people who're really interested in dreams, aren't they?"

So Mr Byculla had consulted Dr Lessing, and shown himself unexpectedly, and indeed incomprehensibly, pleased with his new acquaintance.—"But you are right," he told Sir Simon, "when you say that he is worried. He has many worries. He is a man, I think, who has always been unhappy, and now he has made himself more unhappy because he has learnt too much and yet not enough. I like him most awfully!"

There, then, was another bond between them, though tenuous and not to be compared with the rich and dusty continent that was their common ground. India was the vast foothold of their friendship, and their knowledge of its ceremonies and temples—of princes and ascetics, of gipsies and usurers and God-intoxicated Thugs—of the Gods themselves, blood-boltered Kali forever dancing, and the little-eyed Ganesh—held them, as if it were a herring-net, by the knotted cords of an inclusive interest.

In the afterglow of India's burning plains was forged, against all likelihood, an intimacy so deep, yet easily accepted, that Mr Byculla, without offence, could even demand of his patrician host, "What have you got—you, in your present circumstances—to live for, Sir Simon?"

CHAPTER FIVE

AN affluent widow, sadly perplexed by the nullity of her existence, had revealed, on Dr Lessing's sofa, the identical quality of her grief for a dead husband and her sorrow for the loss of a Sealyham terrier; and confessed with lugubrious relish her unrequited passion for a middle-aged hairdresser from Streatham. Dr Lessing had listened patiently, and said good-bye to her with a weariness that seemed to have become almost palpable, that pulsated in his mind.

He opened the window and breathed a cold sunlit air. There had been frost in the morning, the first frost of autumn, and a red sun above the haze. Then, in the afternoon, the still air was suffused with a golden light, a veiled and gentle radiance, and gleaming window-panes shone yellow like dead leaves. Nature's autumnal gifts, if one were free to accept them, were more to be prized, he thought, than the bouncing, over-many favours of the spring. Spring out-grew its welcome, falsified its promise; spring prospered and turned vulgar in July. But October never stayed long enough, and made no promises at all. October spent itself quietly and richly, the tall trees bowed farewell, and the great rains came down to wash the dead fields for their winter funeral.—But it was too soon to think of winter, and ungrateful to autumn's bounty. He had an hour of freedom, and but for their Austrian maid the house was empty, for Claire had promised she would take the child to the park . . .

He opened the sitting-room door, and saw Claire, a couple of cushions at her back, lying on a sofa. Her shoes lay, where she had kicked them off, on the floor beside her, and she was reading a library copy of an American police-romance. "Hallo," she said. "Taken some more easy money?"

"I thought," said Lessing, "that you were going to take Clarissa to the park?"

"Yes, I meant to, but she got into one of her difficult moods, so I put her to bed."

"But on a fine afternoon like this——"

"You saw how she was at lunch, and you know perfectly well that when she's like that you can't do anything with her."

"She wouldn't eat, I know; but that was because you'd given her some chocolate an hour before."

"It's my fault again, is it?"

"I think you might accept responsibility for your actions; that's all.—But at the moment that's not the point. The real point is that it's a fine day, and a run in the park would have done Clarissa a lot of good."

"I suppose I was to carry her there, kicking and screaming?"

"She's quiet enough now. . . . There's nothing wrong with her, is there? Did she want to go to bed?"

48

"I gave her a soothing powder."

"So that you could be at peace! Do you think medicine's prescribed for the patient or the nurse?"

"I tell you the child was screaming——"

"Because, in the first place, you had neglected a very simple set of rules that I drew up——"

"Do you seriously expect me to live according to your rules and regulations? To order my life as you think proper? To give in to you, and wait for your word of command? Because if you do—well, the sooner you go and see another psychiatrist the better!"

Lessing, his cheek-bones showing white through his skin and his mouth twitching, controlled his anger—Claire stood in her stocking-feet, half-shouting at him—and said in a trembling voice, "If you can't understand that it's wrong, profoundly wrong, to get your own way by drugging a child, then it's quite clear that your life should be ruled by someone."

"Oh, for God's sake talk sense and stop being melodramatic! Who's drugged a child, I'd like to know? All I did was to give her a soothing powder——"

"A powder that contains a small amount of chloral hydrate, which, on the authority of the British Pharmacopoeia, is a drug."

"I know nothing about the British Whatever-it-is, and I don't want to. What I do know is plenty—and that is that you spend your life making mountains out of mole-hills, and condemning everything

D   49

unless you've read it in a book. I've heard about enough of your complaints——"

"Have you ever asked yourself if they were justified?"

"I don't need to, because I know what prompts them."

"Oh really, Claire! You can't seriously believe that everything I say is 'prompted'? That it's directed against you, and all my arguments are arguments *ad hominem*?"

"Oh, go to hell, George! You're bad enough in English, but when it comes to Latin—oh, go to hell!"

There was such hatred in her voice, an extremity of feeling as if she were pouring out the very lees of emotion, that Lessing's anger—no stronger, at its best, than a poor swimmer in a rough sea—was drowned in desolation, and miserably he gave up the fight.

"It isn't far," he said, and stood for a moment or two while Claire, returning to the sofa, pushed up the cushions, smoothed her hair, reopened her book; and, though breathing tumultuously still, put on a stony look of incommunicable deafness.

He went back to his consulting-room, and closed the window; for already the air was colder.—It's getting worse, he thought, but only gradually worse. It can't last for ever, but it may go on for a long time yet. I don't see how to get out, and even if I did . . .

He walked to and fro, head bent and shoulders sagging, till a sudden decision led him to his desk, and sitting down, he opened with nervous, impatient fingers his long-paged day-book.—Work, he said to himself, isn't listed in the British Pharmacopoeia, but it's the strongest of them all, and thank God it's habit-forming.—He took out a loose-leaved, black-bound volume, sharply closed a drawer, and looked for his last week's notes on Mr Byculla. The pages fell open at the proper place, and he saw the envelope he had addressed to Sir Simon Killaloe, after Mr Byculla had left and Claire had gone out. It contained the £5 with which he had intended to pay for his picture of the Thugs and their victim; and he had forgotten to post it.

As though it were a draught of hot and humid air, a flush of embarrassment discomfited him—Sir Simon might even suspect him of dishonesty—and tearing the letter open, he wrote a hasty apology and stamped another envelope, and was about to hurry out and post it, with no more loss of time, when his next patient was announced; and Mr Byculla came alertly in, smiling and assured of welcome.

"Here we are again!" he exclaimed. "Oh, I have been looking forward to this afternoon, for I have some highly interesting things to tell you. Yes, indeed!—And how is your good self to-day, Dr Lessing? You are well, I hope?"

With a tired smile and a perfunctory gesture, Lessing offered his hand. Mr Byculla took it warmly, and stooping a little with the friendliest concern, looked closely at his doctor.

The liveliness of his expression vanished, and anxiety took its place. "Oh, oh!" he said, making a little trumpet of his lips, "but you are fatigued! You have been working too hard. You have been worrying. You need a holiday!"

"Come, come," said Lessing, "you're the patient, not I. I'm allowed to worry if I want to."

"But you have been worrying too much," said Mr Byculla, stepping back a pace or two, and from that distance scrutinising Lessing as if he were a horse of doubtful quality in the sale-ring. "You have been making yourself unhappy."

"That, after all, is my own affair," said Lessing irritably. "The British Medical Council hasn't so far insisted on happiness as a professional qualification—we're short enough of doctors without that—and even though I mismanage my own life, I may still be of use to others."

"Yes, of course," said Mr Byculla, "that I know, that I understand. But I am sorry.—You are not angry that I tell you so?"

"It's very kind of you," said Lessing. There was a little pause, and then, deliberately raising his voice to a higher, more cheerful note, he continued: "But now we've got to think about you and your problems, and I must say that there's no sign of their undermining your general health. You're looking very well indeed. Have you been sleeping better?"

"Till the end of the week, yes. But on Saturday a little nightmare, on Sunday a bigger one, and last night the biggest of all—but also the most interesting. That you will agree when you have heard it.

But I must begin at the beginning, and tell you about the little one first.—No, I do not want to lie down.''

Mr Byculla sat on the edge of the sofa, leaning forward with his elbows on his knees and his fingers pressed together. His expression was serious, his voice sank to a deeper note.—''In the commencement of my dream,'' he said, ''I am stepping into a lift. It is a small lift, big enough for two people only. I close the outer door, and then the inner door, which is made of steel. It shuts *cling-clang*—there is an echo—and then I am in a cage, but it is well lighted. I press a button: I mean to get out at the third floor, and there are five floors only in the the building. The lift goes slowly up, very slowly, and then, between the second and third floors, it stops. I am not much alarmed. A little, but not much—until the light goes out, and then I cry for help. But I shout once only, and I am ashamed of myself when the lift begins to move again. It is still dark between the floors, but I see light above and I am ready to get out. But the lift does not stop! It goes up past the third floor, past the fourth floor, there is darkness again, and now I am shouting properly, and shaking at the steel door; for I am very frightened. At the fifth floor——''

''Did you wake?'' asked Lessing, as Mr Byculla hesitated.

''There were only five floors in the building,'' said Mr Byculla, ''but at the fifth floor the lift did not stop. It went up past the light, and into darkness. It went more quickly now, so quickly that I lost my breath. I was choking as well as screaming, as if I was drowning in the sea; but the sea was the darkness above the world! And then—then I was a little boy again, hiding in a corner and much ashamed—for then I heard *knock, knock,* and a voice at the door. I had been shouting so loud that someone had come to see what was wrong. There was someone knocking at the door.''

"In fact?" asked Lessing. "Or were you still dreaming?"

"I had been dreaming plenty for one night, Dr Lessing. The knocking at the door was real. I had wakened the lady next door, and she was much perturbed. It was highly embarrassing, I can tell you, having to explain to her why I had been making such an unseemly noise.—But on Sunday night, when I had my second nightmare, I made no noise at all. I took good care of that, for I was wide-awake when it happened.''

"You were awake, and dreaming too? That's unusual."

"I woke up the very moment it began. I woke up, and did not know where I was! Everything was strange, and I could not find the cord to put on the light. I was in great haste to get out, but where the door had been there was some large and heavy piece of furniture. So I knew then there was mischief brewing, and steps had been taken to prevent my escape. But I was cunning, I kept quiet, and very quietly I moved the piece of furniture away from

54

the door.—Then more disappointment! For behind it was only the bare wall! I was quite aghast, but keeping my head I crawled a little farther, and presently I put my left hand into a hole, where it was held fast. And then I knew where I was.—Yes, I had found my shoes, just where I had left them, and a moment later I turned on the light and saw that my bedroom was in great confusion. I had pulled a chest of drawers away from the wall, and my bedclothes were so much disturbed that perhaps I had been sleeping in quite the wrong direction. I felt most awfully foolish when I saw where I was, but all the same I was much relieved to be there."

"I think," said Lessing, "that your second nightmare presents no great difficulty."

"But my desire to escape was persistent even after I was wide-awake and crawling round the floor!"

"You were probably only half-awake. And there's a simple explanation——"

"All right, all right. If it is so simple, let us say no more about it. But explain to me, please, why last night I was trying to let someone else escape!"

"That was in your third nightmare?"

"And much the most unpleasant, though I myself was in no sort of dangerous predicament at all. No, far from it. This last time, I was on the outside! I was outside some municipal park, or botanical garden perhaps, that was surrounded by a high railing, and inside there was some creature prowling about and desperate to get out. I, too, grew desperate to let it out. I was going to and fro, shaking the railing just as I had shaken the door of the lift, and looking in vain for a gate. But there was no gate, and the creature inside—I do not know if it was a man or some sort of animal—was running through the bushes, now crying loudly, now mewing or whimpering. It was terrible!''

''What happened?''

''I pulled out some railings, and fell down. Then it jumped over me. I could not see what it was, but it was bigger than I had thought.''

''Perhaps,'' said Lessing, ''the third nightmare was not so radically different from the others as you suppose. The predicament, in all three cases, is approximately the same, and the main difference appears to be that in the first two dreams your role was passive, or relatively so, while in the third you were an active agent. Now——''

''You mean, do you, that it was I myself whom I was trying to release from the botanical garden? But no, it did not feel like that.''

''It's not impossible, however.—But the dreams, of course, can't tell us everything we want to know. They're very interesting, and I'm sure that in a manner which we can't as yet properly define they're suggestive. But to discover what they do suggest, or hint at, we shall have to use other means. And now I'm going to add a line or two to my notes, and—you do smoke, don't you?—you might like to have a cigarette.''

A minute or so later, Lessing said, ''When we first met you told me that you'd served, during the war, as a secret agent in Eastern Europe and the Levant. You were in fairly constant danger, I take it?''

''Oh no!'' said Mr Byculla. ''For most of the time I was bored quite stiff.''

''But there must have been occasions when your work was dangerous?''

''Now and again, but not often. Once, when I was in prison, they tried to frighten me, but I did not pay much attention.''

''Were you long in prison?''

''For ten days in Graz, for three months in Pleven. That was all. And each time I was arrested on technical charge only. They knew nothing. It was all right.''

''But you must have found it an alarming experience?''

''No, no. I sleep very well in prison.''

''Well, that's true philosophy, I'm bound to say. —And then, when the war was over, you decided to live a life of independence, on your own means?''

''I have private means, yes. But a little money does not give the right to say, 'I am my own master.' ''

''It helps, however.—And now what I want you to do is very simple, very simple indeed, but usually it requires a little practice. I want you to lie down— that's what the sofa's for—and relax in every limb, as though you were going to sleep; and then let yourself talk of anything that comes into your mind.''

"You want me to raise the floodgates and let out the stream of consciousness," said Mr Byculla comfortably.

"Yes," said Lessing, somewhat disconcerted. "Yes, I do."

"I am very good at that. I invented it while I was in prison, and practised it every night as the most convenient way of inducing slumber.—But you must tell me where to start from. How shall I begin?"

Lessing, not wholly at his ease, looked about him and caught sight, on his desk, of the envelope addressed to Sir Simon Killaloe. "With a five-pound note," he said.

"Why a five-pound note?" asked Mr Byculla, sitting up.

"It's the first thing I thought of," Lessing explained. "Anything will do for a start."

"Money," said Mr Byculla, lying down again, "is the root of all evil. Or so they say. But that is too loose an explanation, and what they mean is either an immoderate desire of money or an immoderate lack of it——"

"I'm afraid that won't do," Lessing interrupted. "You are arguing, you see, and argument isn't what I wanted."

"No one ever put himself to sleep by thinking about money," said Mr Byculla.

"Then let's take something else. Something quite different. A prison cell."

"There was a policeman," said Mr Byculla, "with a wart on his cheek-bone. It was the biggest

58

wart I have ever seen. It was dark brown and the shape of a volcano. Like Mount Etna in Sicily. I have seen it smoking, I saw it once send up a smoke-ring as if there was someone inside, a giant, I suppose, smoking a huge cigar. A cigar with a band on. That is a joke I used to like very much when I was quite a small boy: to smoke a cigar with abandon. But my father got tired of it in no time at all. He had high-class taste in literature as in everything else, and could not stomach a pun. But if we are to talk of stomachs, it is my mother's I should tell you about, for it was truly remarkable——"

"No!" exclaimed Lessing. "That's no use at all. You're not here to entertain me! You mustn't think of subjects. You mustn't think at all, but talk at random without paying attention to what you're saying.—Now try again, and start this time with your father."

"My father," said Mr Byculla obediently. "My father when he is dying. It was very difficult for him. He was usually a most religious man, but very often he used to change his religion. And now when he is dying he cannot remember what he believes in. He has been a Christian many times. A Buddhist twice, I think. Once he believed in the Bab, or Bahaism: that lasted for more than a year. Then Herbert Spencer, because he declared that pleasure was an inexpugnable element in morality.— The Coptic Church disappointed him, but he was devoted to Bergson for a little while, and being also a Polytheist he read the Rigveda with pious attention.—But now, on his death-bed, is he perhaps a Moslem? He cannot remember, and religion, he says, should be like a Hindu wife of the olden time: with you in life and with you in death . . ."

Lessing, with close attention and a persistent doubt, listened to his patient for nearly half an hour. To all appearance Mr Byculla was as deeply relaxed, as oblivious of another's presence and off-his-guard, as any psychiatrist could wish to see him. He had unbuttoned his jacket, his hands lay placidly on his stomach. His sallow face looked soft and plump, as if he were half-asleep, and his heavy breathing was an audible accompaniment to his soft, slow-spoken sentences. But much of what he said was too interesting—well, not too interesting to be true, Lessing admitted, but so much more lively and entertaining than the usual running of the turned-on tap, that it suggested, sometimes strongly, the conscious art of a good story-teller rather than half-conscious, all-untutored memory. And then, when Lessing had at last decided to stop the suspect flow, it shrank to a mere trickle of isolated phrases and reluctant words; and dried up altogether like a bath-tub gurgling empty. Mr Byculla, sound asleep, was gently snoring.

Lessing woke him five minutes later, and Mr Byculla sat up, yawning. "That is precisely how I used to send myself to sleep in prison," he said. "And now I am feeling much refreshed, though my throat is dry after so much talking.—Tell me, what is the time?"

"Five minutes past six."

"And I am your last patient for to-day?"

"You are."

"Then let us go out together and have a drink. I have been talking too long, you have been listening too long, and you were already tired when I came in. It is a drink, or perhaps two drinks, that now we need. Come on, Dr Lessing!"

"Well," said Lessing, glancing at the inner door while memory looked back at his late quarrel with Claire—Claire with whom he must patch up yet another uneasy truce—"Well, there's something to be said for that."

"Then let us go. I will take you to a nice place."

"Then give me a minute," said Lessing, putting away day-book and loose-leaved case-book, and slipping the letter to Sir Simon into his pocket, "a minute to wash my hands.—You too, perhaps?"

"No, thank you," said Mr Byculla. "I am quite comfortable."

CHAPTER SIX

MR BYCULLA called a passing cab, and opening the door, pressed a genial hand on Lessing's shoulder and pushed him in. "To the Ritz," he said.

"The Ritz?" Lessing repeated. "I hadn't expected such grandeur."

"I have a theory," said Mr Byculla, "that nowadays, when you want a drink, it pays you to go to the best places. The cheap places are no longer cheap, they do not all give you good measure, and their liquors are often of poor quality. But the best places, though they are more dear than ever, do not swindle. You get good measure, and your cocktail is highly potable. So I go quite often to the Ritz—but not to eat, only to drink. I have another theory about food. In due course, perhaps, you will also come and see if I am right about that."

Checked only for a little while at Oxford Street, their cabman drove without hindrance down Davies Street and into Berkeley Square; but when he turned up Hay Hill, to swing with sudden cornering through Grafton Street into Albemarle Street, Mr Byculla moved impatiently and looked at his watch. "They will never go directly, these drivers," he complained. "They have their favourite routes, they consider themselves and not the passenger."

"There's one-way traffic in Dover Street," said Lessing.

"Yes, I know. I know that, but one-way traffic merely encourages them to be most wilful; and I dislike being hurried when I am having a drink. It is now six-twenty."

In the Ritz bar Mr Byculla ordered two large dry Martinis, and when they were brought, said peremptorily to the waiter, "Bring two more, if you please, of the same sort and size."—The second pair being delivered, he let out a deep breath of satisfaction and exclaimed, "Now for half an hour we can relax! Now we can be as much at ease as your patients when they are lying on the sofa, Dr Lessing.—But do not let us talk about your patients; you have had enough of them. Tell me if you know any of these people here. I am interested in people."

"I'm afraid I don't," said Lessing. "This is a much grander *milieu* than I'm accustomed to——"

"Not all of it," said Mr Byculla. "Not those two, for example. They are not at all grand, though he may perhaps have a lot of money in his pocket."

"Well, that's the difference. My friends have not."

"But your patients? Some of them are grand?"

"Only one or two. I see most of them at a clinic where they pay little or nothing."

"Yes, yes, you are a good man. I saw that from the beginning.—Tell me about yourself. How did you come to be a psychiatrist?"

"I think," said Lessing slowly, "that the impulse, towards something of the sort, has been in me since boyhood. I wasn't a happy child——"

"But neither was I!" declared Mr Byculla. "What man, who deserves our interest, was happy in his childhood? I was not, and you were not! Did you hate your father?"

"No, I revered him. It was a stammer, a dreadful stammer almost inhibiting speech, that made me unhappy . . ."

He drank his second cocktail, and in an atmosphere that had mysteriously become congenial and friendly—he looked round him, from time to time, and could not remember a homelier or more harmonious environment—he recited the tale of his troubled youth to a confidant who, not patient only and passive in companionship, provoked him by sympathetic questioning to the remembrance of long-buried circumstance and details, all unhappy, lost in a most resolute oblivion. Not until their third Martini, but now a small measure only, was set before them did Lessing perceive some incongruity in his situation; and then, with half a giggle, and the faintest protest, said, "I say, dear fellow, this is going too far!"

"No, no," said Mr Byculla. "It will be far enough, and no more. Before dinner it is good to have two or three cocktails. So drink up—not too quick, but not too slow—and then we shall have dinner together. Let us make a night of it!"

"But I ought to be going home. My wife will be waiting for me."

"You are not hen-pecked, I hope?"

"Oh no, far from it. Nothing like that, I assure you. But you know how it is——"

"I know also how it should be! A man is master in his own house, is he not? He telephones to his wife and says: I am coming home for dinner!—She is overjoyed, and makes him welcome.—Or he says: I shall be late to-night, do not wait for me. And she is much cast-down, but answers: You know what is best, my dear.—Is that not how it should go?"

"Well, that is the ideal, perhaps, but in practice it doesn't always work out exactly so. Not exactly."

"To-night," said Mr Byculla, "the actual must coincide with the ideal. Go and tell your wife that you are dining with me."

Lessing finished his cocktail. "I think I will!" he said, and suppressed a nervous laugh. "It'll be quite a surprise for her."

Mr Byculla showed him where he could use a tele-phone and said, "When you have finished you will find me outside, on the steps by the main entrance from Piccadilly. I like to breathe the night air. But do not hurry, we have plenty of time. It is now four minutes to seven."

Lessing, squaring his shoulders and gathering his wits, spoke through the telephone with unusual de-cision, and with uncommon detachment listened to

66

Claire's immediate complaint that he would ruin her whole evening and make nonsense of her labour to prepare a meal for him. . . . He interrupted her with a brusque assurance to which she was quite unaccustomed, and putting down the receiver went to get his hat and coat. He joined Mr Byculla on the steps above Piccadilly as Big Ben, its notes coming softly on a south-east wind, was chiming seven; and cheerfully remarked, "Well, I soon settled that.— But look! Don't you recognise him?"

A tall figure, walking briskly under the arches, had passed on the dark pavement below.

"Wasn't that Sir Simon?"

"It may have been. I did not observe him closely. —But come now, let us take some exercise and walk. And presently I will demonstrate my theory of eating."

Mr Byculla's taste was eclectic. From the Ritz he took Lessing eastward to Piccadilly Circus, and thence by Shaftesbury Avenue and Charing Cross Road to Oxford Street; where, with a pride as large and exclusive as if he had discovered the source of the Brahmaputra, he pointed to Messrs Lyons' Oxford Corner House.

"I found it myself," he declared. "No one had told me about it. No one! And the food is good— you will see for yourself—and the helpings generous. It is, moreover, much less costly than the Ritz.— Let us make haste, for I am hungry."

Though the restaurant was numerously and noisily occupied, Mr Byculla seemed oblivious of his many neighbours, and when they had been given a table, looked about him with a happy, proprietorial air. "You see this?" he asked, passing a menucard to Lessing. "You can take your choice, absolutely. You can have Fried Fillets of Lemon Sole with Tartare Sauce for two and ninepence, and then a Risotto Bolognese for one and threepence or Roast Shoulder of Lamb with Baked Beans and Roast Potatoes for one and eightpence.—But do not pay attention to the price, for it is my treat.—And afterwards, perhaps, you would like a Chocolate Marshmallow Sundae, or a Coffee Marshmallow, or both. I myself invariably take both, I am so fond of all sweet things."

Stimulated by his meal, during which he talked incessantly, Mr Byculla then proposed that they go to the second house of the Palladium; for which, indeed, he had already bought tickets. Lessing, who had no wish to go home, agreed with but little persuasion, and, infected by his companion's gaiety, laughed as heartily as he at clowns and jugglers; and thoroughly enjoyed himself.

The night was fine, and Lessing decided to walk home. He thanked Mr Byculla most warmly for such generous entertainment, and still stood talking, their hands clasped in a prolonged good night, on the pavement by the Oxford Circus tube-station. Mr Byculla seemed reluctant to leave him. "It is my pleasure to give happiness," he said. "It is how I enjoy myself. And we shall have more good jaunts together, I hope. Perhaps next Tuesday, if the night is propitious and the weather suitable? Will you be free, Doctor?"

"Yes—but next time you must be my guest."

"That is all one to me."

"Well, thank you again—and good night!"

"Good night, Doctor. Good night!"

CHAPTER SEVEN

On the following evening, after dinner at the Beauvoir Private Hotel, Sir Simon Killaloe and Mr Byculla went upstairs to the latter's bedroom, and Sir Simon was once again persuaded to take the armchair. Mr Byculla with proper solemnity brewed coffee in a glass retort, and unlocking the recently acquired sea-chest in which he kept his brandy, poured out two tots of scrupulous equality and handed one, with a little bow, to his distinguished guest.

"I've been reading Sleeman again to-day," Sir Simon said, "and I found his story as fascinating as ever."

"You mean Sir William Sleeman? The officer who put down all Thugs in India?"

"That's the man. You know his book?"

"Of course. It is most important."

"A certain genius, and a vast patience: I suppose that's always the reformer's strength. But the Thugs themselves——"

"They were as patient as Sir William Sleeman."

"I wonder if their victims ever suspected them?— Take a case, a typical case, of a traveller, a pilgrim perhaps, going slowly in the fashion of the time to Nasik or Benares. He falls in with a couple of

71

strangers, who show themselves friendly. They are going in the same direction, they tell him, and in various little ways they help him along. They are unexpectedly kind to him——''

''In India,'' said Mr Byculla, ''kindness is not unexpected. If you are a traveller, a pilgrim, it is what you look for in every village. No one, in India, would suspect a stranger of evil intention because he had been kind and charitable.''

''Not even in the days of Thuggee? It was the usual thing, remember, for a Thug to ingratiate himself with his victim: sometimes, indeed, with a most convincing parade of sympathy he seems to have made himself almost indispensable to the poor wretch whom he intended to murder and rob as soon as the time was ripe and he had found a suitable place for assassination.''

''It was not so simple as that,'' said Mr Byculla with a sigh. ''There was also a religious motive, and I myself, in my small and superficial study of the subject, have convinced myself that a Thug's sympathy for his poor dupe may often have been quite heartfelt and sincere.''

''But murder and robbery were always the end in view,'' said Sir Simon. ''That murder had a certain religious significance I don't deny and I don't doubt; but the religious impulse was neither pure nor single. The Thugs made their living by murder.''

''It was thought, perhaps,'' said Mr Byculla, ''that the murderer is worthy of his hire.—I am putting forward excuses, you understand. My attitude is the same as yours, of course, but theirs was quite dissimilar. It is necessary to make allowance."

"They were devotees of the goddess Kali; and she is not a goddess for whom I have much liking."

"But she is, nevertheless, the symbol of an essential factor in life. Destruction is a part of nature, just as much as creation. Siva her husband is fertility, and black Kali, dancing on his ribs, is death. They are complementary, Sir Simon."

"I feel that death should be less exuberant."

"But why? In England you picture death as an old man, coming quietly, with long beard and no flesh on his bones; but in India they see a black woman, dancing and grinning and kicking her legs in the air.—Is your old greybeard a more truthful vision?"

"We have grown accustomed to it."

"In India, Sir Simon, they had grown accustomed to Thugs, until Sleeman put them down. And the Thugs were not old men with beards, creeping and crawling by the roadside, but young and hale. You yourself have a picture——"

"It was among those I sold; though I haven't been paid for it yet."

"I am sorry.—But you remember, no doubt, the position of the principal or leading Thug in your picture: he has approached his victim from behind, he has thrown his *pagri* in a noose over the victim's

73

head, and lifting high his bare foot he sets it against the victim's back, while with a smart pull he draws *pagri* towards him, thus breaking the unfortunate fellow's neck. Now an elderly grey-beard, suffering perhaps from rheumatoid complaints, could not procure death so expeditiously as that.''

"The usual method of killing was simpler, I think. It was merely strangling or garrotting. They used a turban, or a bow-string, or a rope, and throttled their victims.''

"To break the neck, to be swift and give no pain, was the habit of the best practitioners,'' said Mr Byculla with a gentle melancholy in his voice. ''And the real artists of the profession used only their bare hands.''

"Where did you learn that? I've read all the available books——''

"You have doubtless read Sleeman's *Ramaseeana*, and Fryer, who does not tell you much, and Forbes, who is no better——''

"But Sherwood and Thornton are good, and both are fairly copious.''

"They make many mistakes.''

"What reason have you for saying that?'' asked Sir Simon, a little tetchily.

"For one thing, they do not know what I have just told you: about breaking the neck. But you yourself could do it in the proper way. You have a thin body and long legs. Long thighs—they are most important. I will show you.''

74

Mr Byculla stood up, and moved the bedroom chair. He raised his left leg so that his thigh was parallel with the floor, and from the knee the lower leg hung straight. Slowly he brought his knee upward and in towards his chest, his foot closing with down-pointed toe to meet his groin. He was unexpectedly supple, and the length of his thigh was remarkable. He stood straight, chest and thigh in apposition, and his knee came within a hand's breadth, or a hand and a half, of his collar-bone. "You also could do this," he said. "Get up and try."

"Forty years ago I could," said Sir Simon, "but I'm rather too stiff for it now, I'm afraid."

"Try," repeated Mr Byculla; and a moment later —"There! I told you so. You are almost as good as me. It is a long thigh that is necessary.—And now, stand behind me, put your leg up again and press your knee against my back. Reach forward, and place your hands round my forehead, clasping your fingers lightly."

"I can't quite manage it," said Sir Simon with some discomfort in his voice.

"Press more closely against your thigh—but look, Sir Simon! In the glass. Is it not risible, I ask you?"

The reflexion in the long glass of a mahogany wardrobe, of Sir Simon, a little embarrassed but intent on securing a neck-breaking grip, and Mr Byculla, his tall frame arching slightly back, was as ludicrous indeed as frogs at their nuptial exercise;

75

and Sir Simon, flushing and clearing his throat, returned hurriedly to his arm-chair.

"It's interesting as an experiment," he said, "but all I've demonstrated is that I'm much too old for high-class Thuggee. My man would break loose long before I got my grip."

"The pull with the hands, the pressure with the knee, must of course be simultaneous," said Mr Byculla. "But you can see how easy it would be for a young man who was sufficiently agile and had practised his profession."

"What I really want to know is where you got your information. I thought I knew all the sources."

"Let me give you a little more brandy," said Mr Byculla. "After your exercise you must require some refreshment."

"Only a small one.—Are you going to tell me?"

Mr Byculla, sipping brandy, was silent for perhaps a minute, perhaps longer. His face fell into heavy lines, as though his cheeks felt the weight of ponderous thoughts within. From the depth of his chest he drew a sigh that was almost a groan, and said, "I am breaking faith with my father if I tell you. But after all, why not? It is true that he forbade me to speak of the manuscript; but for what reason, I do not know. My father, though a religious man, was not averse to shady practices if they promised to be of benefit, and he may have acquired the manuscript by theft. If so, he would naturally wish me to say nothing about it."

"What was this manuscript?"

"Well," said Mr Byculla, growing suddenly cheerful again, "in for a penny, in for a pound! I will tell you all about it.—It is not a long manuscript, about sixteen pages only. It is entitled: *Statement by Hanuman Chand, a Thug from Sankal, now condemned to death. Taken down and translated by F. G. Nisbet in Jubbulpore, November, 1832.*—Much of it is very dull, telling in most tedious detail how he had become acquainted with one Sasanka Mohan Das, a money-lender, and accompanied him on a journey of fourteen days before killing him. He had but small expectation of profit, for Sasanka Mohan Das, it turned out, was indeed a *rara avis*. He was a money-lender whose clients cheated him, and he was almost destitute. But then comes a highly interesting passage: Hanuman Chand describes the way by which he killed his friend, and Mr Nisbet has made a little drawing to show quite clearly that he used only his hands and his knee. And this, says Hanuman Chand, was how his father taught him, who was very strict in his profession and would use only the best methods.—So there, Sir Simon, is the information at my disposal."

"Have you still got the manuscript?"

"It is in Beirut. I have a small house in Beirut."

"That's your home, is it?"

"It is a roof under which I keep some books, a good carpet from Khorassan, and a few pictures including a blue Picasso that my father bought dirt-cheap. But there!"—Mr Byculla pointed to an old-fashioned Gladstone bag and a smart leather-and-canvas hold-all.—"There is my home as much as the house in Beirut. I am a most restless person, merely a vagrant upon earth."

"I wish you had brought the manuscript with you."

"Had I been able to foresee such great good fortune as meeting you, I would assuredly have done so."

"Is it your authority for saying that the Thugs felt a certain pity for their victims?"

"That is true statement, Sir Simon."

"I don't deny the possibility of that, but what's your authority? It's not a generally accepted view. I doubt, indeed, if such a thing has ever been suggested before."

"Nevertheless and notwithstanding, it is a veritable fact, and since you demand to know, it is on Hanuman Chand's testimony that I say so.—Hanuman Chand was observed in the very act of doing to death Mr Sasanka Mohan Das, over whose body he was heard to exclaim, '*Mujhe afsos hai, Sahib, lekin ab ap sidhe raste men hain,*' which means: I am sorry, sir, but now I have set you on your proper road."

"Yes, that's roughly the translation."

"Mr Nisbet, who wrote down his statement after his capture and trial, was much interested in this farewell to a dead man, and by good treatment of Hanuman Chand won his confidence. Hanuman Chand told him that he had thus saluted every one of his victims, and such was the invariable custom of his father and all other Thugs with whom he was acquainted."

"Well, yes. One could read a good deal into that if one wanted to, of course, but I don't think a jury would accept it as proving that Hanuman Chand's motive was pity."

"The concluding pages of Mr Nisbet's manuscript," said Mr Byculla, "are a *catalogue raisonné* of the seventeen people whom Hanuman Chand had previously done to death. There are brief notes on each person, and it is clearly evident that all were wretched sufferers in this vale of woe. Calamity of one sort or another had sorely stricken them. They had been the target, as Shakespeare says, for innumerable slings and arrows. And Hanuman Chand, in releasing them from life's torment, had been activated by purest pity. That is what he swore to Mr F. G. Nisbet."

"I don't believe a word of it," said Sir Simon. "I know a good deal about India, and to me it just doesn't ring true.—Now you mustn't be offended, for I'm not disputing your good faith. No, not for a moment. But I do question your Mr Nisbet's judgment. What probably happened, as it seems to me, is that he showed too much sympathy to Hanuman Chand, who promptly saw a chance of escaping punishment for a lifetime of crime if he could dress it up in high-falutin sentiment. And Nisbet swallowed his story hook, line, and sinker.—Good heavens, man, have you ever seen a pi-dog dying in

79

misery in an Indian village? And does anyone ever think of putting it out of pain? Of course they don't. They let it lie, and leave mercy to the blue-bottles. And if they won't take the small amount of trouble that's necessary to shoot a dog, why should they accept enormous difficulties, and the risk of hanging at the end of it all, to give his quietus to an unhappy man?—No, no, it won't wash. I like Indians, and I enjoyed their company for nearly forty years; but you're not going to persuade me that altruism is one of their dominating qualities.''

''Man,'' said Mr Byculla gently, ''has a soul, and that is the difference between man and a pariah dog.''

''It won't do,'' Sir Simon said again, and stood up, tall and frail and obstinate. ''Those fellows made their living by it——''

''So do the priests of every faith,'' said Mr Byculla. ''But it is not often a rich living.''

''In a way that's true, I suppose, but it would lead us into all sorts of argument, and I think we've had enough for to-night. I've enjoyed the discussion——''

''Don't go yet. Have a glass of brandy.''

''No more. I mustn't acquire extravagant habits: I've got to watch my step nowadays.''

''I have not offended you, Sir Simon?''

''Far from it, my dear fellow. You've given me a most interesting evening; and our disagreement, after all, will make an excellent excuse for resuming

the argument later in the week.—But don't ask me
to practise Thuggee again. I'm too old."

"You are too kind, Sir Simon."

"Good night."

"Good night, Sir Simon."

CHAPTER EIGHT

On the following Sunday, a day of short-lived, honey-coloured light within still canopies of mist, there was, in the Lessings' flat, a domestic upset of unusual character. George Lessing was surly, unreasonable, and petulant; while Claire was sensible, sympathetic, and conciliatory. And Clarissa, the child, playing with quiet good humour, did nothing to exacerbate dispute.

The morning began lazily, in comfortable untidiness. Having breakfasted, they sat in a growing litter of Sunday papers, their attention idly held by week-end politics and the theatre, by literary opinion, gossip, and crime in turn. Claire, from time to time, said, "I think I'll take Clarissa to the park"; and Lessing with languid approval would reply, "Yes, that's a good idea." The breakfast dishes were still unwashed, for their Austrian maid, who cooked, cleaned, and received Lessing's patients with a bland and smiling grace, was free for the weekend; but she had left a cold steak-and-kidney pie in the larder, and Claire's mind bore no burden of kitchen difficulties. A cigarette-end, unregarded, smouldered in an ash-tray, and the air grew a little stuffy. But the air was peaceful. No bitter words, no angry waving hands disturbed the blue stem of

83

wavering smoke that climbed, and flowered, and disappeared; but amicably Claire exchanged the *Sunday Express* for the *Observer*, and Lessing thought: In the morning, without her make-up, you can see the fineness of her bone, and when she keeps it low her voice is good.

Then the telephone rang; and neither feeling any interest, each waited to see if the other would get up to answer it. It was Lessing who gave in.

"A trunk-call," he said, a moment later.

"It may be your mother," said Claire.

He spoke more loudly: "Yes, I'm George. Don't you know my voice yet?—It's Harriet."

"I told you so."

"*What?*"

"What's the matter?"

"Oh, be quiet.—Yes, I can hear you perfectly. Go on . . . I want you to tell me exactly what happened, and then, if the doctor's there now, I'd like to have a word with him . . ."

Claire, in a nest of newspapers, listened bleakly to fragments of Lessing's conversation with his sister, but his share in it consisted of little more than questions, harshly uttered, and she could not gather from them what sort of calamity it was that had upset the household in Shrewsbury. Then he asked her for a cigarette, and said, "She's gone to fetch the doctor to speak to me."

"But what's happened?"

"My mother fell downstairs this morning and

84

broke her leg. Right femur, high up near the joint. She's in a bad way and a difficult mood.''

"I knew it was something like that! As soon as the telephone rang, I felt sure it was your mother——"

"Hullo! Yes, this is Lessing speaking . . .''

His voice became professional, and for a few minutes he discussed with apparent calm his mother's accident and the management of her case. But when he put the receiver down, he spoke with unconcealed anger.

"If I've told her once,'' he said, "I've told her a dozen times to be careful on that stair. It's more like a trap, an oubliette, than a staircase. And now when she has fallen, as I always knew she would, she's in a state of hysterical obstinacy and refuses to go to hospital. Patterson—that's her doctor—says he daren't insist on it, in the condition she's in, but he's very doubtful if he can get a nurse. And Harriet isn't being much help.''

"You'll have to go, won't you?''

"We've got the Harrows coming in to-night, and I particularly wanted to see him; and there's the clinic to-morrow, and two patients in the afternoon.''

"But a broken leg, at your mother's age——"

"Yes, it's dangerous.''

"My mother's Aunt Janet fell in the same way, and never recovered. The shock was too much for her. But she was eighty.''

"Mother won't die, not for a long time yet.''

"But if she did, and you weren't there, you'd never forgive yourself."

"Oh, I've got to go, I realise that. But it's an infernal nuisance—and you know what I'm like after a couple of days under her roof."

"I'll look up the trains," said Claire.

Moving with the quiet and unobtrusive efficiency of a well-trained nurse, Claire gathered and folded the untidy newspapers, and found a time-table; while Lessing stood in sullen resentment and made no move to prepare for his journey.—So long as he was in London, and his mother in Shropshire, he not only felt a genuine and most kindly regard for her, but could believe himself bound to her by natural affection. In memory, and at a distance, her character had the attraction of a well-played comic part: her arrogance could not hurt, her high-pitched stupidities had a certain grandeur, her intermittent shrewdness and her unexpected cruel perceptions gave liveliness and colour to her role. No one had ever complained that she was dull, and she wrote excellent letters that revealed all her stubborn folly, her irremediable presumptions, and the bitter perspicacity that never failed to surprise as well as wound. Lessing delighted in his mother's letters, and every week took pains to send her in reply as much sharp comment and bold opinion as he could muster.

But he could hardly endure to be in the same room with her for more than an hour or two. For an hour she would be as entertaining as her letters, but then, either wilfully or by chance, she would utter some intolerable criticism, pass upon a friend insufferable judgment, and mounted on her arrogance maintain her view with brutal insistence; and come down next morning to raise the ghost of last night's argument, and harry it afresh. She lived surrounded by enemies whom she despised, and who made submission to her, twice a year or so, for the pleasure of hearing what she had to say about their neighbours. Lessing, after he had stayed with her for two or three days, would forgive her more quickly; but always, when he returned from Shropshire, he brought with him a recurrence of the painful stammer that had spoiled his youth.

Claire got on surprisingly well with old Mrs Lessing, and would frequently protest how much she admired her. Claire, when she pleased, could be quite indifferent to insult, and from her rude mother-in-law she had won grudging recognition of her toughness. Claire's stupidity was sometimes equal to Mrs Lessing's, and occasionally their shrewdnesses were also parallel. It was Claire who had discovered, by deduction and busy but discreet enquiry, that her mother-in-law was a wealthy woman; and astonished George Lessing with her news. He, who had no financial acumen, was at first unwilling to believe that his mother had anything more than a barely comfortable income; but was finally convinced by the evidence that Claire had marshalled. Then, for a little while, he accepted the fact of her wealth as another facet of her theatrical character, and took no heed of its implications for himself until Claire, by foolish repetition of the sum she had estimated, and her frequent reference to his mother's age, betrayed her greedy interest in what would presumably be his inheritance.—It occurred to him, then, that by her death his mother might do him greater injury than ever before. For Claire, with money in the bank, would make abominable and destructive demands on him, and his quiet seemly practice would be ruined by her appetite for display. Claire on a modest allowance was difficult enough; Claire with money to burn would be intolerable.—And now he must go, to put up with his mother's company, to make a show of filial affection against her hysterical ill-humour, and while his torment grew, so would his fear that she might die and make him rich.

"Your train goes at eleven-ten," said Claire, "and gets in at three-twelve. You'll have to hurry. Shall I pack for you?"

He denied his inner feelings, and gave voice to superficial annoyance. "I was looking forward to seeing the Harrows to-night," he complained. "There are half a dozen things I want to discuss with him."

"You can have lunch with him later in the week, when you get back."

"Yes, but that won't be the same."

"I know, dear. It's terribly upsetting, but your poor mother will be waiting for you. What do you want me to pack?"

"Oh, a suit of pyjamas and a clean shirt: that's plenty."

"Don't you think you should take a larger suitcase, and your black clothes—just in case?"

"For God's sake, stop talking like a ghoul!"

"I didn't mean to do that," she said, keeping her temper, "but naturally I'm worried——"

"Yes, yes."

"Well, I'll put some things in your week-end bag, and you'd better wear your tweed suit. If you do need anything else——"

"I shan't."

"I do hope you're right!"

"I shall be back to-morrow afternoon. I'll stay the night in Shrewsbury and make sure that everything possible is being done for Mother's comfort. —A chance to bully me will do her as much good as anything, I expect.—And then I'll get hold of a nurse somehow or other, and leave her to it. I can't do more than that."

Claire packed, and Lessing changed the flannel trousers and homespun jacket he was wearing, not for the tweeds that Claire had sensibly advised, but, in wilful rejection of her choice, for a dark London suit. Wallet and watch, handkerchief, eight or ten shillings in silver—he felt in his pockets, a little fretfully, as an absent-minded man does, never quite sure that he has everything he will need; and found a letter addressed to Sir Simon Killaloe.

"Oh, God!" he exclaimed, and realised with dismay that it must have been there for the better part of a week. Since Tuesday, in fact, when he and Mr Byculla had had an evening of pleasure.

"What's the matter?" asked Claire.

"I've found a letter that I forgot to post. I haven't worn this suit for the last few days."

"Is it important?"

"Not really, I suppose, but—oh well, it can't be helped. I'm going to look for a cab."

He went out, holding the letter in front of him, as if on a salver, and posted it grimly at a corner pillar-box. He stopped a cab, and found that Claire had already carried down his week-end case, his over-coat, and a couple of magazines for him to read in the train. She charged him with messages of love to his mother, and made him promise to ring her up, and tell her the latest news, at night. With an anxious look on her face she kissed him good-bye.

She returned to the flat, and sitting on the floor played for a little while with Clarissa. "What a good girl you've been!" she said. "Let's go for a walk in the park; would you like that?"

She dressed the child, and leaving her with a newspaper to tear, put on her maquillage and shoes, and a Sunday morning hat. But before leaving the house she paused and thought a little, shrugged her shoulders, and took up the telephone.

"Ronnie?" she said. "Are you up yet? Well, listen.—George has had to go to Shrewsbury, his old mother's had an accident, and I'm just taking

Clarissa for a run in the park. But we'll be back by about half-past twelve, and there's a little gin in the house. So if you'd like to come in and have a drink, and stay to lunch if you've nothing better to do . . .''

CHAPTER NINE

ALWAYS a methodical man, Sir Simon had imposed upon his life an order that grew ever stricter as his activity diminished and purpose became obscure. An exact routine allowed him to watch his small expenses and reduce them little by little to conform with narrowing circumstances; but also, and more importantly, it gave a semblance of dignity and meaning to an existence that had become pathetically aimless. He took comfort in routine, and resented interference with it.

On Monday morning, however, he decided to postpone his usual reading in the British Museum, and see his solicitors. The post had brought him— as well as Lessing's overdue letter, with a £5 note in it—a cheque from Messrs Sotheby for the collection of Persian, Moghul, and Hindu paintings which they had sold for him. The pictures had brought a good price, but hardly so much as he had hoped; and he was uncertain whether it would be sufficient to pay off the expenses of Ronnie's trial, for which he had accepted responsibility. He had been waiting for the money with a contained and bitter impatience to discharge his debts, and disengage himself from a sordid association; and now, to settle everything if he could, or, at the worst, to discuss his remnant liability and how to meet it, he telephoned to his lawyers to ask for an immediate appointment, and by half-past eleven was sitting, in a periphery of deed-boxes and documents, in a dark office in Lincoln's Inn. The conversation that ensued was long and difficult, and when it was finished Sir Simon had to reconcile himself to being somewhat poorer than before. His solicitor, an old friend, took him out to lunch, and thereafter Sir Simon went to the British Museum, to read again Sleeman's essay on Thuggee.

He left the Reading Room at half-past four, according to his custom, and going by tube from Russell Square to Piccadilly, walked to his club in St James's Street. He ordered a pot of tea and toast, and read the papers until a quarter past six, when he drank a whisky-and-water and gossiped for half an hour with two fellow-members, both older than himself. At five minutes to seven he left the club and walked to the tube station at Green Park, beside the Ritz Hotel. He took train to Gloucester Road, and at sixteen minutes past seven walked upstairs to his room in the Beauvoir Private Hotel. He opened the door and was surprised, then angry, to find Ronnie there.

Ronnie was studying, with no apparent dislike, his reflexion in the looking-glass on Sir Simon's dressing-table, and smoothing his black, oiled hair with a heavy, ivory-backed brush.—Sir Simon, his annoyance audible in a harshly indrawn breath, ex-

94

claimed, "Put it down, please. The brush! I may be old-fashioned, but I do prefer to have the exclusive use of my hair-brushes."

"You've nothing to worry about," said Ronnie. "I'm not a leper."

"I made no charge against you. I spoke only of my own wishes.—Have you any particular reason for coming here?"

"Well, there's nothing unnatural, is there, in my wanting to see you now and again?"

"Your visits aren't generally inspired by mere affection."

"You mean I never come to see you unless I want something?"

"That is putting it more crudely."

"I've come to you when I was in trouble, I know that. And you've got me out of trouble. More than once. And I'm grateful."

"I'm delighted to hear it."

"I've earned a lot of black marks in my time, but you can't accuse me of ingratitude."

"Is this leading up to anything?"

"I wish you wouldn't make things so difficult!— But you've never sympathised with me, have you? I don't suppose you can. You've been lucky in your life, you're irreproachable——"

"That is too much to say of anyone."

"I've done things that I'm sorry for, but you can look back at your life without regret, without shame——"

"Do you really suppose that's true?"

"Well, your reputation hasn't suffered, like mine has."

"I may have been more discreet.—But what does this talk of reputation imply? That yours is under yet another cloud?"

"No, it isn't, and it isn't going to be! It's just the other way about. I've got a chance at last. A good chance."

"Then I hope you'll take all possible advantage of it."

"Yes, I'm going to. My God, I'm going to! And that's what I want to talk about."

"You want my advice?"

"Well, I want you to feel interested, to begin with.—You see, there's a friend of mine, a first-class fellow called Hay, who's in touch with a big American manufacturer of motor-car accessories——"

"What are they?"

"Oh, heaters, and cigarette-lighters, radio-sets, driving-mirrors, and that sort of thing. There's a tremendous market for them, and this American firm's going to start a factory here. Well, Hay's got the chance of an agency, and wants me to go in with him."

"It doesn't seem to be essential work, but technically, I suppose, it's honest?"

"It's more than that, there's money in it. Real money! I'm absolutely sure that I could repay you in six months' time——"

"Repay me?"

"We've got to raise five hundred pounds to get

the agency. Hay's all right: he can put his hands on two or three hundred without any trouble, he says, and if you can let me have two hundred and fifty——"

"No," said Sir Simon.

"As a loan! A loan for only six months!"

"I'm neither going to lend you money, nor give you money. You have cost me too much already."

"But this is different from anything I've ever put up to you before. This isn't going to cost you anything. I tell you, there's an enormous market waiting for these American accessories, and I've got a chance to get in on the ground floor——"

"Listen to me, Ronnie. I can't afford to lend you two hundred pounds, because the lawyers have very nearly cleaned me out. The lawyers, I mean, who were responsible in one way or another for defending you against a charge of murder."

"But I was innocent! That wasn't my fault."

"I never doubted your innocence, and because I believed in it I undertook to have you properly defended. But your defence cost me a great deal of money, and I cannot afford another two hundred pounds for a project that seems to me as improvident and scatter-brained as all the other schemes you have devised for making an easy living.—No, don't interrupt me, I haven't finished yet. I was going to say also that even if I could afford to give you such a sum, I wouldn't do so. I'm going to give you nothing more, because everything I have ever given you has been wasted. Throughout most of your life, from your schooldays onward, you have shown yourself to be utterly unreliable, idle, untruthful, and dishonest. You've caused me untold pain, and brought disgrace on a name that has been associated, for a good long time now, with decency and public service. You had a chance, in the war, to prove you were better than we had been forced to conclude, and you refused to take it. You got thrown out of a good regiment because your courage was dubious, and about your morals, unfortunately, there could be no doubt at all. Then you enlisted in the ranks —and for that I gave you credit—but instead of redeeming your character, you deserted. Since then——"

"I'm not going to listen to any more! I didn't come here to be lectured as if I were a child. I've had enough of it.—If you were to die to-morrow, and I lived another fifty years, all I'd remember about you would be that you'd never given me an hour of sympathy! Never anything but damned Victorian pulpiteering!"

For a moment or two, as they stood facing each other in their anger, their physical resemblance was remarkable. Tautened and flushed by rage, by disappointment, Ronnie's tired and dissipated features matched, though fleetingly, his father's patrician scorn; and his lean body in its shoddy suit was a smaller image of the older man's spare and upright figure. But the stiffness of his anger did not long endure, and when its force weakened he threw himself into the arm-chair by the bedside, in a lost, ungainly attitude, and began to cry.

Sir Simon, in a cold embarrassment, turned away, and taking off his coat and waistcoat, laid them on the bed. "You had better go now," he said. "My quarters are somewhat confined, as you can see, and I have to wash, or I shall be late for dinner."

"You can't throw me out like this! I'm penniless."

"You have heard what I had to say, and I don't intend to repeat it."

"I'm not going till you give me something!"

Sir Simon took off his shirt, and removing the cuff-links, dropped it into a basket. "If you insist on staying," he said, "you will have to put up with the unpleasant sight of my ablutions. I'm sorry to be so discourteous, but the pinch of poverty does lower one's standards."

"You can make a joke of it," cried Ronnie, "but what am I going to do? I'm penniless, I tell you. I'm down to my last ten shillings."

"There's no lack of work in the country. You had better give your name in to some employment office," said Sir Simon; and turned on the taps of the wash-hand basin.

"To get a job as a casual labourer, I suppose?"

"You have no technical ability, and you're not trustworthy: what else can you expect?"

With soapy hands and head bent low, Sir Simon vigorously scrubbed his face and neck, and Ronnie, leaning forward and watching him with wary eyes, slid his fingers into the inner pocket of his father's jacket, that lay on the bed beside him. He could feel a note-case, an envelope of soft leather without latch or fastening, and with the smooth skill of a cardsharper he drew from it three notes, new and stiff to the touch, and one that was soft and folded.

"You'll be sorry for saying that!" he cried, and stood up with his right hand in his trouser-pocket.

"There's no need to wait," said his father, and filled the basin with cold water. "I can hardly be sorrier than I am already."

"All right, if you want me to go, I'll go," said Ronnie, and stood for a moment by the door. "But I'd like you to know that it's you who've driven me to this, and—oh, what's the use of talking!"

He went out abruptly, closing the door hard behind him, and Sir Simon, after drying his face and hands with scrupulous care, took a clean shirt from a drawer. He heard the dinner-gong, and felt sick at the thought of food, and people eating together. But his looking-glass, as he brushed his hair, reflected a face as smooth and hard as old ivory.

CHAPTER TEN

MR BYCULLA was walking through a grimy, yellow-ish air to his usual Tuesday appointment. The fog, that had slowly been investing and descending upon London, now lay, reinforcing November's early dark, on invisible roofs and filled the streets with an acrid cloud in which lamps glowed with a pretty travesty of light. Mr Byculla, with confident step and cheerful bearing, walked up Welbeck Street, and presently arriving at Dr Lessing's door, was greeted by Ilse, the smiling Austrian maid, with the disconcerting news that the Doctor was out of town. He had had to go to the country, she said, to see his mother, who was seriously ill. That was on Sunday, she explained—talking German now, for Mr Byculla had prompted her with a question in her own language—and though he had been expected back this morning, he had not yet returned.

"But this is most unfortunate," said Mr Byculla in German almost as fluent as Ilse's. "I am greatly upset. I had felt assured of seeing the Doctor to-day."

"What a pity!" said Ilse. "I am so sorry. And the Doctor, he too will be disappointed when he is told that you came here to no purpose. He is a man who takes everything to heart. He would never neglect a patient of his own accord.''

''Do you think there is any chance that he will still arrive this afternoon? Is there not, perhaps, another train?''

''That I do not know,'' said Ilse, ''but I will enquire. Take off your coat and sit down, and I will ask Mrs Lessing.''

Claire, with a cigarette between her lips, came out of the sitting-room and said, ''Mr Byculla? I'm so sorry that my husband isn't back yet. I couldn't ring up and warn you not to come, because I really expected him, and he himself definitely intended to be here by lunch-time.''

''And now,'' asked Mr Byculla, ''there is no chance whatever that he will come to-day?''

''I'm afraid there isn't. He was telephoning just before you came in to say that he's got to spend another night in Shrewsbury. He's with his mother, you see. She fell and broke her leg, and at her age that's very serious, you know.''

''It is never a nice thing to happen,'' said Mr Byculla gravely.

''No, it must be terribly painful; and then there's the inconvenience, of course.''

''That applies to many things,'' said Mr Byculla. ''That Dr Lessing should be absent to-day is for me highly inconvenient. I had been looking forward very much to seeing him, and after his professional care he would, I think, have come out with me for a few drinks and a little jollity.''

"You took him out to dinner last week, didn't you? He enjoyed it so much. And now this wretched business has upset your whole evening?"

"The best-laid schemes of mice and men," said Mr Byculla, "are almost always going astray."

"Well, if you're quite at a loose end, why don't you stay and have a cup of tea? Ilse will make some more, won't you, Ilse?"

"*Bitte sehr!*"

"*Besten Dank,*" said Mr Byculla. "*Wirklich zu nett von Ihnen!*"—And to Claire: "That is most kind. I should much like to have tea with you."

"You speak German, do you?" she asked. "I couldn't understand a word Ilse said, when she first came."

"In Beirut, where I live for some of the time," said Mr Byculla, "even small boys on the street speak three or four languages. Not well, of course; only a little bit. But one learns what is useful."

He had her laughing a minute or so later—laughing too loudly, to cover her surprise and some small embarrassment—over a story of youthful precocity in the Levant; and not long after he was suggesting that she, since Lessing was not there, should come out and drink with him. "At the Ritz," he proposed. "They make good cocktails there. I have a theory about drinking, that one should drink only at the best places. But I will tell you about that later on. Now you would like to make yourself ready, no doubt?"

"But I hardly know you," said Claire, compressing her lips to a forbidding line and looking him up and down with overt speculation.

"I did not know you at all when I came in to tea," said Mr Byculla, "but I was not frightened."

"Well, I should think not!"

"I do not ask you to come to some low dive. The Ritz is highly respectable."

"It couldn't be grander——"

"That is almost what your husband said. And he enjoyed himself when he came."

"But it's so foggy to-night."

"There is not too much. I have good eyes in the dark, and we shall find a cab very soon."

"Well, only for a little while," said Claire. "Just for half an hour!"—And with the condescending smile of a schoolmistress giving way to a child's eager but foolish request, she retired to her bedroom.

Mr Byculla sat alone, thoughtful and very still, for twenty minutes. Then Claire returned, her complexion now fresh and ardent, so smartly dressed and briskly scented that she brought an image to the mind of a frigate, newly painted, leading an aggressive fleet before a favouring gale. "I haven't kept you too long, have I?" she gaily enquired.

"No, no," said Mr Byculla, looking at his watch. "We have plenty of time. It is now a quarter to six."

"I do hope we find a taxi."

"We will," said Mr Byculla. "I am always lucky."

He opened the door for her with a slight inclination, like the mockery of a bow, but on the threshold she was halted by the ringing telephone. "Oh, damn the thing," she exclaimed. "But wait a minute, do. I must answer, it may be George. About his mother, you know."

"Hullo," she said, and looked suddenly impatient and out of humour. "Well, I'm sorry, but you can't come now. I'm going out. . . . Yes, George is still away. . . . Not for very long, but I can't say exactly when I'll be back. How could I? . . . Oh, don't be tiresome, Ronnie. I'm not being unsympathetic, but I was just on the point of going out. . . . Yes, you can ring again, I shan't be late. . . . I'm sure you are, but everybody's worried nowadays, so don't make too much of it. . . . All right, I'll remember. Good-bye."

"The telephone," said Mr Byculla, who had been waiting politely in the hall, "is not an unmixed blessing."

"For most of the time it's an utter nuisance," said Claire; and then, when beyond the outer door she encountered the fog, "But I can't see a thing!"

"It is not quite so bad as that," said Mr Byculla, and confidently took her arm. "We shall find a cab, I think, in Wigmore Street. I never fail to be lucky."

Almost immediately his confidence was justified,

but the cabman, grumbling loudly, could rarely make better speed than a pedestrian, and it was eighteen minutes past six when they arrived at the Ritz. There were few people in the bar, and no apparent need for hurry, but Mr Byculla was curiously restive until a waiter brought the large dry Martinis that, without asking Claire's choice, he had immediately ordered; and then, as he had done when Lessing was his guest, he asked for two more of the same sort and size.

"Goodness!" said Claire, astonished. "You might as well be an American! I haven't seen anything as quick as that since they went home. You never knew what to expect in those days, and though it wasn't all fun, of course, I will say this for the war, that it did teach a girl to look after herself.—I don't drink as quickly as this, Mr Byculla."

"But of course not! It is only the first you should drink quickly, and the second one—sip, sip, sip! Quite slowly. Because now you are not thirsty, but you like the taste. It is the same as life, Mrs Lessing. When you are very young, you come out of the door with a rush, you are greedy, your mouth is wide open——"

"Oh, surely that isn't true!"

"I am using figures of speech. It is the best way of talking, to make things clear and interesting too. —In youth, I say, you take life quickly, like a drink when you are thirsty and want a great deal of it. But after, when you have grown up and are no longer in such a hurry, you should enjoy the taste. And so I drink in a way that will remind me of life, and how I am wiser than I used to be. A glass for youth, bottoms up! Another for good sense and pleasure too, *rallentando*."

"What a fascinating idea! I've never met anyone who had thought seriously, like that, about drinking. Most people just drink because they're bored, I suppose. But you make it so interesting."

"You are flattering me."

"Oh no, I'm not! I wouldn't dream of flattering a man. Men don't need it, I assure you; they flatter themselves quite enough. I got to know more about men than I'd ever thought possible—that was during the war, of course, when all of us were doing what we could—and if there's one thing a man doesn't require, it's flattery."

A little shrilly, perhaps, but with great enjoyment, Claire recited for Mr Byculla's admiration her memories of brave days in uniform, when senior officers had sat beside her, day after day on the summer roads of England, captivated by her well-bred profile and the swift dexterity of her driving. Her dashing anecdotes appeared to have a like effect on Mr Byculla; for he listened with exemplary attention, and when the bravura of her stories yielded to a little sentiment, to a sigh for distant happiness, he beckoned to a waiter and said, so quietly as to make no interruption, "Two dry Martinis, please; but small ones now." Nor did Claire notice, so discreet was his movement, that a moment earlier he had looked at his watch.

"Still another drink!" she exclaimed. "Isn't this one too many?"

"No, no, it is only a small one," said Mr Byculla in a comforting voice. "And when we have had this, you will come and dine with me, I hope. It will give me much pleasure."

"But I ought to go home——"

"Why?"

"Well, that's what I intended to do."

"To live always according to intention may become most wearisome. And since you like my good ideas about drinking, you may also approve of my custom with regard to eating. Dine with me just once, as an experiment to see if I am right."

Claire needed little more persuasion, and a few minutes before seven they got up to go.

"The Ladies' Room is there," murmured Mr Byculla.

"But I don't want——"

"There is no hurry, I will wait," he said, and spoke so commandingly that Claire, with more meekness than her habit, obeyed his pointing finger. —But it was she who had to wait, for when she came out, after Big Ben, muffled by the fog, had sounded the ghostly time, Mr Byculla had still to get his coat and hat.

"Let us go out this way, into Arlington Street," he said. "It is the way to find a cab."

"Thank goodness the fog's no worse," said Claire, looking over the shrouded pavement. "Or is it the cocktails I've drunk that make me take a more cheerful view of it? That's the danger of drink when you're driving, it makes you too cheerful. I never used to touch it when I was on a job, except a gin before lunch, perhaps . . .''

Mr Byculla made no reply, but stood silent and abstracted in the yellow gloom. In that light, or lack of light, his face looked hollow-eyed and chap-fallen, like a tragic mask, and it was in a voice of incongruous tragedy that he said—after waiting for less than a minute—''There is no cab here. We shall have to go and look for one. It is this way. Come!''

With a firm unfaltering tread he took Claire across the blindness of Piccadilly, and northward along Berkeley Street into what seemed a vast ocean of fog where there were no landmarks, but above them floated dimly the lights of ships at anchor in the gloom.

Claire, though still buoyant on the gin she had drunk, was becoming aware that Mr Byculla was less responsive than he had been, and a slight feeling of annoyance increased her discomfort in the vaporous dark sea of Berkeley Square. ''I can't see a thing!'' she complained. ''I've no idea where we are!''

''On the east side,'' said Mr Byculla with a sigh. ''It is not yet too difficult. But take care, we are going on to the road now. It is Bruton Street we are crossing. And now again—the pavement.''

''Yes, I can see that much,'' said Claire, resenting a little the manner in which he assisted her, as if she were an old lady; and to show her independence, disengaged her arm from his.

"We come to the corner," he said, now a couple of feet from her, and she turned rather unsteadily.

"Oh!" she exclaimed, bumping against a railing, and stopped to rub her elbow. "Mr Byculla! I can't see you. Where are you?"

There was no answer, and with a sudden anxiety she moved forward blindly, her hands held out for protection, and stumbled badly when again she stepped off the pavement. For a moment she felt wholly lost, and then, on dark-winged memory, came a sharp irrational fear that took her breath away.—She must be, she thought, in that little street on the north side of the Square where weeks and weeks ago the body of the dead girl had been found. Fanny Bruce. Ronnie's girl, the little prostitute who had gone about her business with a dog on a leash. The girl who had had her neck broken. —Her knees trembled, she felt her heart knocking, and the fog came groping round as if to wrap her in impalpable thick cerements, and choke her. She turned in a panic to see who was behind her, and whimpering, ran blindly forward till a voice called "Stop!"

"Stop, stop!" shouted Mr Byculla. "Where on earth are you going to, Mrs Lessing?"—Then, opening her eyes, she saw the dark shape and dim lights of a cab, and a tall shadowy figure on the running-board.

"I saw him in the distance, he had come out of

Davies Street, and I hurried to secure him," Mr By-culla explained. "It was only for one minute I left you. Why are you so upset?"

"I've been silly," she said, breathing like a child after a fit of crying, but struggling to control herself. "I nearly fell, and then I realised that I didn't know where I was, and—and I lost my head for a moment. I'm all right now."

"Yes, you are all right now. Of course you are! Get in and rest yourself, and we shall go and have a good dinner."

Claire paid no attention to the direction they took, nor asked any questions until, with Mr By-culla's hand again at her elbow, she found herself being guided to a table in the Oxford Corner House. Then, unwilling to recognise her surroundings, she enquired with an affectation of bewilderment, "But where is this?"

"It is a place that I found all by myself," said Mr Byculla proudly. "No one told me about it, no one at all! But the food is excellent—you will see!—and they give you splendid helpings."

Mr Byculla had apparently regained all his high spirits, and it was with the happiest air, as of complacent ownership, that he showed her the menu-card. "Look," he said, "you can have Grilled Herring with Mustard Sauce and Fried Potatoes for one and sixpence, and then Veal and Ham Cutlet with an assortment of vegetables for one and sevenpence, or Roast Beef with Spinach for one and nine-pence.—There is nothing too dear, you see.—And afterward there is Chocolate Meringue, Chocolate Marshmallow, Coffee Marshmallow. I myself have always two such delicacies with ice-cream. I am so fond of sweet things.''

''I think,'' said Claire, ''I should like a drink to begin with.''

''But of course! You can have anything you like. What do you choose?''

His generosity, however, failed to re-create the loud cheerfulness with which their evening had begun. Claire made enough conversation for politeness' sake, and listened with some show of interest to Mr Byculla's theories of good living, and to several unusual anecdotes. He ate with a good appetite, but she had none. On his hands, moving above the table-cloth, his curiously large finger-nails were very conspicuous, and twice or thrice they caught her eye and held her attention until, as it were, a little shiver blew across her mind.—Her well-bred nose looked pinched and delicate, and when Mr Byculla proposed a visit to the Palladium, for which he had already bought tickets, she thanked him wanly and pleaded a headache. He realised, with manifest regret, that their evening had come to an end; and paid the bill.

It had begun to rain, and Oxford Street through the dissolving fog shone dark and wet. They had no trouble now in finding a cab, and Claire, touched by a remorse to which she was but little accustomed, put her hand on his sleeve and said, ''I'm sorry for being so dull. I didn't want to be, but

I was feeling tired, I think. And then I got a head-ache.''

"You have been most charming,'' said Mr By-culla.

"No, I haven't, but don't think the worse of me. You'll come and see me again, won't you?''

"I shall at all times be delighted to call on you.'' —And on her doorstep, with a rather ponderous courtesy, Mr Byculla said good night.

Claire, dissatisfied, but glad to be alone again, went upstairs and having let herself in, turned on all the lights. The child was asleep, and Ilse had gone to bed. She took off her hat, and changed her shoes, and made tea. She was yawning, and opening a new packet of cigarettes, when the telephone rang.

"Oh, God!'' she exclaimed, "will this bloody evening never come to an end?''

With bitter eyes she stared and let it ring. But its mechanical insistence daunted her, and angrily taking up the receiver she listened to the expected voice. "Yes,'' she said. "Yes, I thought it would be you.''

CHAPTER ELEVEN

WHEN Ronnie arrived, ten minutes later, he found the door of the flat standing open. He took off his wet hat and dripping waterproof, and hung them on the stand in the hall. He went into the sitting-room, and met Claire coming from her bedroom. She had undressed and put on her shabby woollen dressing-gown. She had cleaned the make-up from her face, and as if deliberately to present as unattractive an appearance as possible, she had daubed herself with a cream that lay, under the light, with an oily glisten on her cheeks and forehead.

"Did you shut the door?" she said.

"Yes, of course."

"What's happened?" she asked, regarding him more closely. "You look dreadful."

"I've had the worst day of my life. I've been in hell."

"Well, you'd better sit down. Do you want a cup of tea?"

"No, I don't. I want to know where you've been all night. I've telephoned to you three or four times. The last time was from a call-box. I've been walking about. It got so bad that I couldn't stay at home."

"What's happened, Ronnie?"

"I'm not sure that anything has, and that's the damnedest part of it.—Where have you been?"

"I've been out to dinner, and that's got nothing to do with you."

"All right. I'm too tired to quarrel."

He sat down, as relaxed and careless of appearance as a drunk man, and the light on his upturned face shaded the wrinkles in its lifeless pallor. Claire watched him, hostile and uneasy, and said nothing. Presently, in a dreary, rather querulous tone, he began to speak.

"I've never had any confidence in life," he said. "I've never seen much purpose in it. It's dirty and stupid and almost meaningless, and we flicker about its surface like beetles or flies, whatever they are, on a horse-pond. But that isn't all. If that were all, it would be easier to understand. And it isn't easy. It's difficult because now and then you meet someone who behaves as if he knew what it was all about, and thought it a fairly reasonable state of affairs. There's my father, for instance. It's only the older people who behave like that, I suppose.—Well, I don't think they're right, of course. I'm not being sentimental about them. But there they are, and you can't ignore them. You've got to believe in them, in a way, though you don't believe what they tell you. And then, if they turn out to be as dirty and bogus as the rest of us, well, it's a hell of a shock. Do you see what I'm getting at?"

"No, I don't," said Claire.

"If you're not going to be sympathetic, if you're

not going to try to understand, there was no use in my coming here.—But there was nowhere else I could go.''

''You'd better have a drink,'' said Claire. ''I got some more gin this morning.''

She went out, and returned in a minute or two with glasses lightly clinking on a tray. ''There's a bottle of gin, half a bottle of imitation French vermouth, and water,'' she said, ''and that's all.''

Ronnie got up, and pouring three fingers of gin into a glass, added a little water and gulped it down.

''If that's how you're feeling, I'd better have some myself,'' said Claire.

''You know my father,'' said Ronnie. ''Do you think he could ever—well, have committed a serious crime?''

''I suppose nothing's impossible; but you'd never suspect him, would you?—No, frankly, I don't think it's likely.''

''Nothing's impossible,'' said Ronnie, ''and that's what cuts the ground away.''

''What have you found out?''

''I don't know,'' said Ronnie, and poured another glass of gin and water.

''You might give me one, when you're at it.''

''Don't drink too much. I want you to listen to me.—You remember what I told you about Fanny Bruce?''

''God, yes. I was thinking about her to-night, in the fog. But go on.''

''I gave her a fiver, that last night, before I left

her. Well, fivers don't grow on every bush, so far as I'm concerned, and I'd noticed the number on it. It was 0 13 575310, the figures climbing up and down again, and it stuck in my mind. But there was no mention, either at the inquest or the trial, of any money found on her, and I didn't say anything about it because I'd come to the conclusion that the less I said, the better."

"But if you gave her five pounds, and when the body was found there was no money on it, that means she had been murdered and robbed. Murdered for her money. That was a point in your favour."

"They wouldn't have believed me. They'd have asked where I got it, and I'd have told them at Harringay. Well, that's the usual answer, and they wouldn't have believed me. So I thought it best to say nothing about it."

"But why are you worrying about it now?"

Ronnie took from his inner pocket a note-case of shabby morocco leather, and from one of its several compartments drew a twice-folded note. "That's what I gave her," he said. "There's the number: 0 13 575310."

"Where did you get it?"

"From my father. The day before yesterday."

"He gave it to you?"

"I went to see him, to ask him if he'd help me to get a job I'd been promised if I could raise two hundred and fifty pounds. Well, he refused, in fact, but he gave me a few pounds to keep me going. And

118

this five-pound note was part of what he gave me. I didn't look at it till yesterday, not particularly, and when I recognised it, when I saw the number, I thought I was going mad. It's the same note, you see.''

''But you can't believe——''

''I don't know what I believe. But I gave her a fiver, then someone murdered her and took it from her, and now I get it back. I get it back from my own father!''

''But if it was he who killed her—oh, but it's nonsense!—and took the money, you can't think he'd give it you! God damn it, Ronnie, he'd still be a gentleman, even if he was a murderer! He wouldn't do that.''

''All right,'' said Ronnie, ''he didn't give it to me. I took it. I took it out of his pocket-book. He wouldn't lend me two hundred and fifty pounds, which I'd have repaid him, so I took what I could get, and that was three pound notes and this fiver.''

''You bloody crook!''

''I'm a crook all right. I know what I am, and I'm past being disappointed. But I believed in him! I didn't like him, but I believed in him. And now——''

''There's some explanation, Ronnie! He may have got it from anyone.''

''He may have got it from her.''

''Not a man like your father. He's the soul of honour and goodness.''

''I said to him on Saturday, 'You've got an

unfair advantage. You're irreproachable.'—'That's too much to say of any man,' he answered.—'You've lived a life without fault or shame,' I said.—'I wish that were true,' was what he replied.—So it may be nothing more than a façade, you see; that nobility of his, that pretence of virtue and dignity. And there's another thing, too, that struck me: he said he'd always known that I was innocent.''

''But you were!''

''Of course I was! But how was he to know, unless he knew who the murderer was?—He'd only my word to go on.''

''And that's not worth much, is it?''

''It has its good days.''

''But why should he murder her? He'd no reason to! You can't pretend he's the sort of man to kill a girl on the chance of finding a five-pound note in her stocking.''

''I wanted to marry her,'' said Ronnie, and helped himself to more gin. ''I told you she was in love with me, but I'm not so sure that I told you I was in love with her. Well, I was. I wanted to marry her, and because I'd never wanted to marry anyone before—no, not even you!—well, I took her to meet my father. I wanted it to be a proper sort of marriage: nothing underhand about it. I didn't tell him she was a whore, and I didn't think he'd see it. But he did. He didn't show it to her, he was very good to her: like His Excellency behaving well to someone he doesn't know, but who's being neglected at a garden-party. But afterwards he let me

120

have it; and it was like a horse-whipping. He asked me if I meant to live on her earnings, and laid it on so heavily that at last I swore I'd never see her again. But I did, of course, and he met us one night. She wasn't on her job, and we were just walking together.—Well, the next day I got a letter from him, a hell of a letter, in which he said he was considering what steps he could take to prevent me from utter ruin."

"I don't see what that proves."

"The best thing he could do was to put her out of the way."

"But not by murder!"

"He'd condemned people to death in India."

"It's madness to think he'd do such a thing.—Give me another drink, Ronnie."

"It's driving me mad to think he may have done it. And if he didn't, where did he get this five-pound note?"

"Well, from anywhere. He might have got it from George."

"How?"

"George bought a picture from him—that thing there—and I'm almost certain he was going to pay for it with a five-pound note. Or perhaps that was part of the price. I don't know how much it cost."

"And you think this was the fiver George sent him?"

"I don't think anything of the sort."

"Well, what do you mean?"

"I mean what I said before: that he might have got it anywhere."

"What are the odds against a note, taken from a whore's stocking, coming into his possession unless he took it himself? But if he did—oh, Christ! I can't bear it!"

"Oh, Ronnie! Poor Ronnie. Have another drink."

"What am I going to do with this damned fiver? I'd better burn it."

"No, don't do that. That's just silly."

"I can't keep it."

"I'll take it, I'll give you change for it."

"I couldn't bear to keep it."

"Of course you couldn't."

Claire got up, a little unsteadily, and going to the table where she had left her hand-bag, said, "I've got three pounds, four pounds, four pounds seven and six. That's all I've got, Ronnie. But I'll give you the rest some other time."

"That's all right. I couldn't bear to keep it."

"No, dear, but I don't mind. I don't mind a bit. Because I don't believe your father did anything of the sort, or ever would."

"I've been sitting all alone, just thinking, till I thought I was going mad. You know what my father is."

"I know him very well indeed. And I think you're making a very big mistake."

"There was no one but you I could come and talk to."

"Well, you're feeling better now, aren't you? Because you're quite, quite wrong, and I'm going to give you one more drink, poor Ronnie, and then send you home."

"Is George coming back to-night?"

"No, he's still in Shrewsbury. His mother broke her leg——"

"Then I'm going to stay here."

"Oh, no! You can't!"

"If you send me away, I'll be lost forever and you'll never see me again. Because I'm lost already. Anybody whose father's a murderer is lost."

"You're drunk, Ronnie. That's what's wrong with you."

"And you're not much better.—You're not much better, are you?"

"You might try to behave decently for once. You're in my house——"

"Don't be high-falutin, Claire. You know what we are."

CHAPTER TWELVE

CLAIRE woke, sick and angry, and remembering the unwashed glasses and the dirty, laden ash-trays in the sitting-room, dressed herself with fumbling haste to clear away the sluttish litter before Ilse had a chance to see it; and let in the morning air. Fear of discovery tormented her—never before had she been so rash—and her head was aching with a reiteration of pain that nagged her for such monstrous folly. Her looking-glass rebuked her without pity.

She came back a little while later with a cup of tea, and woke Ronnie. "You've got to be quiet," she whispered. "We made utter fools of ourselves last night, but so far, I think, Ilse doesn't suspect anything. I got up in time to tidy the room."

"She's an Austrian. It wouldn't mean anything to her."

"You know nothing about her. She's a good girl, she gets up at seven o'clock to go to Mass."

"Well, what do you want me to do?"

"Get dressed, and keep quiet. Don't make a sound. I'll send her out as soon as I can to do some shopping. She likes that. And then you can go."

"I'm in no hurry.—Are there any papers?"

"I'll bring them to you."

She brought *The Times* and *Daily Express*, brushed

her hair again, and left him. With an assumption of careless well-being she made everyday conversation with Ilse; dressed Clarissa, and gave her breakfast. In an hour or so she returned to the bedroom, and found Ronnie, in shirt and trousers, lying facedown on the pillow. The newspapers, in disarray, were scattered on the floor.

"Wake up," she said irritably. "It's time for you to go."

He made no answer, and when she took him roughly by the shoulder to rouse him, he turned a face of childish misery, white and red with weeping, and said, "I'll never sleep again."

"Oh, stop acting," she said. "You talked enough last night, I haven't patience to listen to it all over again."

"Look at the papers."

She picked up the *Express* and saw a heading: DEATH IN PICCADILLY. *Ex-Governor's Fatal Fall*.

"In the worst fog of the year," she read, "Sir Simon Killaloe, distinguished Indian administrator, fell to his death last night at the entrance to the Green Park tube.

"No one observed the accident, but his body was found at the foot of the first flight of steps leading down from Piccadilly. Falling apparently headfirst, the deceased, whose face was contused, had broken his neck . . ."

She sat down on the bed beside Ronnie, and with her fingers ruffled his hair. "And we were getting drunk," she said.

"We were talking about him. That's why I came here, to talk about him. And he was dead before I got here."

"What can I say?" she asked. "It won't do any good to say I'm sorry."

"There's an obituary in *The Times*," he said.

She found page 7, where there was a notice nearly half a column long, and began to read: "Sir Simon Killaloe, K.C.S.I., C.I.E., whose accidental death in yesterday's dense fog is reported elsewhere, had had a long career of unusual distinction in the Indian Civil Service. Born in 1886, the only surviving son of the late Major-General F. G. St. J. Killaloe, V.C., C.B. . . . ."

"No, I hate obituaries," she exclaimed, and threw the paper down. "They're all about great achievements, and all the achievement's over and done with. They take all the meaning out of life."

"I'm mentioned in it," said Ronnie. " 'A son survives him,' it says. They should have added, 'whom he hated and despised.' "

"That isn't true."

"Oh yes, it is. And that's how he had such an advantage over me. I only hated him. And sometimes I hated him most when I felt proud of him. If I'd ever known anything to his discredit—something really shabby—I'd have felt so much easier. I almost wish he had murdered Fanny. It would make me feel easier now."

"Don't start that again, for God's sake."

"No, there's not much point in wondering about

it now. We'll never know.—Well, I suppose you want me to get out while the coast's clear."

He sat up and put on his shoes, and Claire asked, "What are you going to do?"

"I don't think it matters much," he answered. "I don't think it has really mattered for a long time."

CHAPTER THIRTEEN

Dressed for the funeral, Claire studied with a de-
served approval her reflexion in a long mirror, and
decided that a new black hat had been no extravagance. Black suited her, and in a subdued maquil-
lage her features had a chill distinction not far from
beauty.

"All morning," she said solemnly, the funeral
image in her mind, "I've kept thinking that it
might have been for your mother."

"My mother will live for ten years yet," said
Lessing irritably.

"She's been wonderful, I know, but you can't say
she's out of danger yet. Not at her age."

"If I'd had to stay any longer, she'd have been in
danger all right. There was a hypodermic syringe
that tempted me badly one night."

"That's not an attractive remark," said Claire
coldly. "And in any case, this is hardly a time for
joking."

She went out, leaving him to finish dressing, and
he looked for the cylindrical bone nail-file that he
customarily used to open the stud-holes in a starched
collar. He could not find it; and again by habit
sought it next in the leather handbag from which
Claire had just transferred a number of small articles

to a black-silk purse that matched her funeral attire.

There was a little pocket in one side of the leather bag from which protruded a doubled corner of thin white paper.

Curious, he pulled out a folded £5 note, and spreading it open, looked at it in dull astonishment. As if a shutter had fallen, a curtain of bewilderment occluded his mind, and for a moment or two he could not perceive any connexion between the note, which he recognised, and his wife's unaccountable possession of it. He could not, as it were, see the two parties to the puzzle in the same field. He knew the note: it was unforgettably numbered. He had posted it, after long delay, to Sir Simon Killaloe, for whose funeral he was now dressing. And it had returned to him, it had unfolded in his idly inquisitive fingers, out of his wife's handbag. But there was no connexion, there was no relationship, between the note in its first function, and its reappearance.

And then, as the shadow of astonishment grew thinner, he discovered a link, a possible conjunction, most unwelcome to his mind. Sir Simon had a son: a son with whom Claire was too friendly. If Ronnie had been the carrier, like a carrier of disease, it was fidelity he had infected—and streaming from this dire thought, pulsing through his arteries and flooding his chest so that his heart beat painfully against the current, Lessing felt the dark tide of jealousy, that he had often struggled against, now carrying him yet again to its insanely peopled shore; and with a violent effort he turned athwart the stream to make for the better coast of reason. Claire must be given a chance to explain. Claire might have an answer that was innocent enough, and wholly satisfying.

"Claire!" he called, opening the door. "Where did this five-pound note come from?"

"Where did you find it?" she asked.

"In your bag. I was looking for a nail-file——"

"You gave it to me."

"When?"

"I don't remember," she said, smoothing its creases between nervous fingers.—"But yes, I do! It was about two or three weeks ago. I was going out to dinner with Ronnie, and I asked you for some money because I thought he wouldn't have any. But he had, as it turned out, and I spent nothing. But I forgot to give your fiver back to you."

"I gave you five pounds on that occasion," he said, "and you certainly didn't return it, or give me any change out of it. But this isn't the note I gave you."

"Of course it is! If you found it in my bag, it must be!"

"I remember the number of this one," he said, "because I was struck by the odd symmetry of it. And in a freak of fancy I decided to use it to pay Sir Simon for that little picture I bought from him."

"And did you?"

"Can't you understand a simple statement?"

131

"But when did you give it to him?"

"I wrote to him, and enclosed it in my letter."

"Are you sure?"

"I admit that for a few days I forgot to post the letter——"

"And perhaps you had forgotten to put the right note in it!"

"I don't make mistakes of that sort."

"Never?"

"Certainly not about this."

"But you have! You're making a wild mistake! Because this is the note you gave me—I swear it is!—and why you should use it to fasten some obscure quarrel on me, I just can't understand. Unless you're so determined to quarrel that you'll invent an excuse when you can't find one."

Again a kind of darkness descended on his mind, as doubt cast a shadow on his memory and persistent jealousy shook it as if it were a blind in the wind. "When," he asked, striving to keep his voice calm, "when did you last see Ronnie?"

"That night," she said, "when we had dinner together."

"Not since then?"

"No!"

He made no answer, and her defiance grew a little uncertain, a little awkward. She rubbed the carpet with her foot, and said, "He's telephoned once or twice, and asked me to come out, but I wouldn't go. Because I knew you didn't want me to."

"I wish I could remember," he said.

"Oh, George!" she cried. "If only you wouldn't torment yourself with these ridiculous doubts and suspicions! I don't know what you suspect now, but there's no reason for it, whatever it is! If only you would trust me——"

"Yes, yes," he answered, disengaging from encircling arms and removing himself from the threatened kiss. "I'm wrong again," he said, taut with impatience and suddenly incapable of maintaining the angry, fruitless argument. "I'm wrong again, but just now I haven't even time to excuse myself.— I'm looking for that little bone nail-file. My collars are either as hard as flint or as limp as a rag; I don't know what the laundry does to them."

"Here it is," she said, fumbling in her bag.

"I wish you'd leave it where you find it."

"I'm sorry," she said.

He finished dressing, and leaving the flat they drove, in a silence broken only, but unavailingly, by Claire's propitiatory remarks, to the crematorium at Golders Green. A veiled sun shone from a thin blue sky, and about the west door of the chapel, in little groups, stood thirty or forty black-coated mourners who, though widely differing in their physical attributes, seemed to possess a unifying characteristic that, at first sight, was not easy to define.

Lessing, having left his car where an attendant had directed him, got out self-consciously and approached the gathered company with some diffidence; but Claire, instructed as to the hierarchy by six years in uniform, drew herself up and walked proudly as if on parade before commanding but familiar officers. There were no more than half a dozen women there, and none so well dressed as she.

Looking about him, Lessing began to discern and recognise the common quality in Sir Simon's friends; long years of authority and command had marked them. There were tall men and short ones, a former Viceroy towered above the others, and some were old and burly, others slight and trim; but all, without consciousness or effort, held themselves like men apart. There were faces that kept the heat of the Indian sun, and lean jaws and sallow skins, and great imperial bony cheeks; but also there were small and gentle men, slight of stature and mild of aspect, and their mildness was sustained by a confidence as sturdy as the easy pride that stiffened the tall ones, the old lions, and the sallow men with black eyebrows and broad shoulders. A great service had used them all; authority had set its seal upon them all.

They spoke, while waiting to go in, in low voices, as if impersonally; and Lessing, to begin with, heard only the close-lipped murmur of their speech, though Claire, with confidence unabated by knowing no one there, had led him into the midst of the largest group. But then, as nervously he stood among them, phrases more clearly sounded, and his hearing was attuned to sentences that joined together in his mind to make a sort of threnody . . .

"That was the world he knew, it's gone for ever.

And no one cares. And no one cares. I met him first in Dera Ismail Khan. I knew him in Madras. A riot in Jullundur, and he put it down. They said he was too friendly with the Mahasabha once. But Jinnah trusted him. And he spoke for the Untouchables. He started well, in the old way, touring in bullock-carts, he knew the people. He knew the country, from Bhutan to Malabar. He built two hospitals, three schools. He built a road. Brought water to the desert. When he was quite young he said a court of justice must be like a polo-field, open for all to see and level ground to play on. They said, at one time, he was too friendly with the Moslem League. But both the Nehrus trusted him. And he spoke for the Untouchables.—Well, no one cares to-day. No, no one cares. The world he knew, the world he lived for, has gone for ever——''

''My dear Doctor! And Mrs Lessing too!'' exclaimed a more familiar voice. ''I am so glad to see you! I have been looking everywhere, but nowhere could I perceive the face of any close acquaintance until by good fortune I spotted you! How happy I am to meet you—in so far, of course, as one can be happy on so melancholic an occasion.''

Among the other mourners, Mr Byculla made an oddly conspicuous figure. He was correctly dressed, but dressed so as to suit a wedding rather than a funeral. His top-hat was surprisingly glossy, his trousers were boldly striped, and in his buttonhole he wore a white chrysanthemum. Somewhat incongruously, too, he carried a small square parcel neatly wrapped in brown paper.—Lessing, without reserve, was pleased to see him; but Claire, more sensitive to the occasion, smiled coldly and withdrew herself a little.

Mr Byculla lowered his voice. "It is a highly distinguished company that has come to pay last respects to our poor Sir Simon," he said. "Not a large gathering, but most elevated. Yes, indeed!— You look beautiful, Mrs Lessing, and you, Doctor, are very well dressed. That is your own suit, no doubt?"

"Well, yes," said Lessing.

"I have had to hire mine for this special occasion. But no one, I think, could detect that it had not been made to order. It is a perfect fit, is it not?"

There was a little exodus of mourners from the chapel—mourners at an earlier ceremony—and presently a verger, discreet of voice and movement, came to summon the waiting congregation. They went in, treading with careful quietness, and saw in a front pew the bowed shoulders of Ronnie Killaloe, in his shabby blue suit, and, decisively apart from him, the upright figure of Sir Simon's daughter-in-law, for whom he had had no liking either. A bishop, old and tall and lean, formerly of the Province of India, conducted the service in a voice like the wind crying among bended trees. "Thou fool," he said, "that which thou sowest is not quickened, except it die."—And Mr Byculla, sitting between Lessing and Claire, emitted a little fluting murmur, like the ghost of a whistle, and nodded his head as if in melancholy but profound agreement.

"It is sown a natural body; it is raised a spiritual body," said the bishop; and Lessing, wondering if that could be true, began to think about his patients and forgot Sir Simon. St Paul, he thought, had been on firmer ground a few sentences before, when he wrote, "All flesh is not the same flesh . . ."

The coffin, under its canopy and pale wreaths of flowers, slid away like a ship being launched, and the congregation waited for Ronnie and his unfriendly, upright sister-in-law to lead them out. His sister-in-law found friends, to whose condolence she replied in a voice of loud assurance; and a few of the oldest mourners, who had known Sir Simon nearly all his life, spoke briefly and with manifest discomfort to Ronnie. But most of them, walking briskly and with obvious relief, went directly to their waiting cars.

Claire said doubtfully, "Do you think we should give Ronnie a lift?" But Lessing brusquely refused, and invited Mr Byculla to drive back with them. Mr Byculla, who had clearly been waiting for such an offer, accepted with alacrity, and as though he were now almost a member of the family, went upstairs with them to the flat, talking amiably the while, and with a manner of some ceremony presented to Claire the neatly wrapped, brown-paper parcel that he had carried to the funeral. She opened it, and discovered a box of Turkish Delight.

"It is my favourite sweetmeat," he declared, accepting a piece that dusted his lips with its fine sugar. "And this, you can depend on it, is the best sort. It was sent to me by a business acquaintance in Beirut."

"But we can't take all this, if you're so fond of it," said Claire.

"No, no, I have plenty more. I am rarely without it," said Mr Byculla, waving with a handkerchief some sugar from his knees; and began to talk, with a bland assurance of interesting them, about his favourite delicacies and Levantine cookery. Claire, attentive to all he said, flattered and encouraged him; for she had no wish to be left alone with her husband—it was Saturday, and he had no more appointments—who would, in all probability, return after fumbling hesitation, but then with unhappy persistence, to the perilous topic of the £5 note. And Lessing, with a dread almost equal to hers, for he knew that he could not avoid the subject and yet shrank from the wrath and recrimination it would arouse, Lessing too was glad, though less openly at first, of Mr Byculla's company; and was equal, at last, with Claire in pressing him to stay.

They talked of Sir Simon for a long time. Claire made much of her tenuous relationship to him, and Mr Byculla's eyes were unashamedly abrim with tears when he spoke of their evenings together in the Beauvoir Private Hotel. He could not, he said, bear to live there any longer, for now it would seem intolerably lonely. He had given up his room, and tomorrow he was going to the Charing Cross Hotel.—

"For a few days only, of course," he explained, "until I have discovered a more congenial site for a residence of some duration. But where that will be, I cannot tell. I am a wanderer, Mrs Lessing. I go to and fro upon the earth, I am a most restless man."

She pressed him to stay for supper, and he agreed on condition that they would accompany him thereafter to the Palladium; for which, as it happened, he had already bought tickets.

"In those clothes?" she asked.

"Why not?" he demanded. "I have paid rent for my suit for a whole day!"

He looked down at his boldly striped trousers and added, "You must lend me a grey tie, Doctor, and then, if anyone wonders, he will doubtless conclude that I have been to a wedding."

CHAPTER FOURTEEN

LIKE thunder in the offing—thunder growling in the hills, threatening always to strike the valley but, as though timorous of the open, still keeping to the upper slopes—suspicion darkened and discomfited Lessing's mind, but could not find the strength, or courage, to unloose the lightning and strike its meditated prey. All Sunday, through its idle hours, he was conscious of the twice-folded Bank of England note in his pocket-book, and miserably aware of its implications.—From himself to Sir Simon, from Sir Simon to Ronnie, from Ronnie (it was obvious, despite her denial) to Claire: and in that passage was the flagrant evidence of her lies and infidelity. But was the passage certain? Could he be sure of its beginning?

Again and again he tried to recapture, in a clear image, his memory of the evening when he had hesitated, with two £5 notes in his hand, as to which he should give to Claire, which to keep to pay Sir Simon for the little Hindu picture of a Thug. He had kept, he thought, the one that was numbered with such uncommon symmetry; but could he trust his memory? He had forgotten—twice he had forgotten—to post Sir Simon's letter, and his memory having been at fault in one respect, could he rely upon it in another?

This doubt, this toothache of dubiety, kept him from charging Claire, once more, with lies and the presumption of adultery, but could not mitigate suspicion nor comfort him against it. He laboured between a cowardly wrath and craven fear—wrath that he dared not yield to, fear of her confessing all he feared—and like a castaway among the savage crests and sucking hollows of a wild sea, said nothing for lack of breath.

Nor did Claire speak of what equally obsessed her. She could risk no mention of the ill-omened note, to ask if he remembered who had given it to him, for fear of worse questions in reply.—Claire's fear was colder than her husband's, more expectant, more like a lonely climber benighted on high snow beneath a curious and staring sky, who dare not cry for help lest an avalanche should tumble down. She, knowing the treachery on which she walked, dared make no reference to her path, and prayed—to gods in whom she had no faith—that Lessing would not speak of it. Claire was no idle traveller, but saw a happy destination in old Mrs Lessing's wealth; and because Ronnie had now endangered her chance of reaching it, her anxious mind, throughout that sombre and splenetic day, was like a pair of nervous hands picking rags of anger and malice to make a patchwork hatred of him. With angry memory and revolt she recalled the submissions that he, and he alone, had forced upon her; with aversion she thought of his weakness and good looks, the shallow charm that had unarmed her, and let spite, like a night-frost, strike and blacken them.

Shortly after six o'clock, Lessing went out. He had promised, he said, to call on his colleague, Dr Harrow. They had to discuss the agenda for the next meeting of a committee on which they sat, he explained with squeamish invention; but all he did was to walk aimlessly about the streets, preferring empty pavements to the dark tension of his overcrowded flat. About half an hour later, Ronnie telephoned from Brighton.

He had gone to Brighton, he said, because he wanted to consider everything clearly and dispassionately, and he found that difficult to do in London.—His voice was roughly confident, and Claire, her lips tightening, guessed that he had been drinking. He was staying, he said, with his friend Hay in a small hotel.

"How could you afford to go to Brighton?" she asked.

Ronnie laughed, and became more self-assured.— There's plenty of money in the world, he told her boastfully; you've only got to find out where it's kept.—He had gone to the undertakers who were arranging his father's funeral, and met someone whom he had known as a quartermaster-sergeant in Cairo, during the war. They had had a little conversation, and Ronnie had borrowed £15 on account of a £20 order for wreaths which, though they would not be supplied, would be charged against his father's estate.

"My God," said Claire, "what a cad you are!"—
And thought, as she spoke, how often she had said it
before, and how little it had meant to either of
them.

"One's got to live," answered Ronnie, self-
congratulatory; and then, more seriously, "Is
George there? Can I speak to him?"

"No, he's gone out. Why do you want to talk to
him?"

"That's what I was going to explain to you.—
Well, you know what I've been worrying about, and
it's just occurred to me that George is the man to
help me, because George is a psychiatrist."—He was
slurring his sibilants a little.—"He's the only
psychiatrist I know, so I'm going to talk to him
about my father——"

"You're not coming to talk to George about anything!"

"Oh yes, I am! You can't stop me. And I'm going to ask him, quite openly, as a psychiatrist, if
he thinks it possible or impossible, or probable
or improbable, that my father murdered Fanny
Bruce."

"Ronnie, you're drunk! Oh, you're worse than
drunk! You must be going mad if you think——"

"Shut up!" he cried, his voice blaring in the receiver. "Don't talk to me like that! I'm not mad,
and I'm not going mad, because I'm taking good
care not to. I don't intend to live like this, thinking about him all day and half the night, and never
knowing the truth of it. I'm going to take steps.

I'm going to find out. Well, George is a psychiatrist . . .''

Claire, holding the receiver a hand's breadth from her ear, listened to him with diminishing attention. —I can put a stop to this, I could bring him to his senses in half a minute, she thought. It was George who sent his father the note. I've only got to tell him that . . . But my God, I'm not going to! It wouldn't prevent him from coming to see George. He would come as soon as he could, quicker than ever, to ask George if he remembers where he got it. And he would tell George he had given it to me, for £4. 7s. 6d. He wouldn't forget that. And then he might as well tell him everything.—Oh, God, let him go mad, stark mad, rather than that!

But Ronnie's voice was quieter and sounded more reasonable now, though there was little enough reason in what he said. ''I've been talking it over with Hay,'' he told her, ''who's a damned good judge of people, and he's had a lot of experience too. He says you should never go by anyone's appearance, especially if it's respectable. He says he knew a Baptist minister once, who looked like a saint, and he's absolutely sure that this minister had murdered his mother and was planning to murder his wife and daughter, but he got run over by a bus before he could do it. It was after talking to Hay that I decided to see George, and ask him, as a psychiatrist, what he thought about my father.''

It may be nothing but a drunken impulse that made him ring up, thought Claire. When he's sober and realises that they couldn't meet without his admitting, or half-admitting, what we've been to each other, without betraying me and accusing himself—that's what'll count!—he'll think again, he'll change his mind . . .

"Ronnie," she said, "will you promise to do nothing about it until you hear from me? Tell me your address, and I'll write to you to-night."

He was stubborn, but at last she got a grudging assent. Not trusting his word, however, she stayed indoors all the next day; but he neither telephoned nor came to the flat.

CHAPTER FIFTEEN

"In this dream," said Mr Byculla impressively, "I am more frightened than ever before. It is a bad dream, but very remarkable. I do not think anyone else could have dreamed it."

"Let me hear it," said Lessing.

"It is more difficult to tell than the others, because it is quite simple, but the figures in it are not like figures that we know. In a way that I cannot describe they seem to be very old; I do not mean old in years, I mean of some older creation, when life was more big and moved quite slowly."

"How does the dream begin?"

"I am on a kind of embankment, a causeway that is raised above the neighbouring country, which is quite flat and like a swamp. There is someone walking close behind me, but I do not know who it is. Sometimes I think it is my father, sometimes I think it is a schoolmaster who taught me mathematics, and sometimes—but I do not wholly like to tell you this, Dr Lessing."

"Go on."

"Sometimes I think it is you."

"Yes, I can understand that, though I hadn't expected it. Not yet. But you needn't worry about it."

"Well, I am walking on this high causeway, and it is still almost dark. The sun has not yet risen, and I cannot properly see the country on either side. In the distance there is jungle, I think; but I am not sure. Nearby, on one side especially, there are grey patches or lumps, like rocks and boulders, on the dark swampy ground. I think they are boulders until I see that some of them are moving a little. And then I know they are people who have been asleep, and are now waking. But they are not people like us. They are too big."

Mr Byculla wiped his forehead with the handkerchief that he kept, in an old-fashioned way, in his cuff; and continued his story.

"There is one who is very broad and thick. He gets up slowly, and looks at me. He does not come closer, but I am extremely frightened, and I walk now with great reluctance because my knees are shaking.—But then I see another, who is tall and thin, but as heavy as the first one. He seems to drag himself from the ground, as though his legs were held in the swamp, and his arms hang down like the broken branches of a tree. If he stood upright he would be enormous, and now it is light enough for me to see that his face is like stone, and his eyes— ah, but I am terrified then, for he is coming towards me, and I seize the person who has been walking behind, and hold him in front of me like a shield. He also is very frightened, and I am ashamed to tell you, Dr Lessing, who he is."

"Myself?"

"Yes, I am afraid so."

"Don't upset yourself about that. What happened next?"

"The broad and thick figure, who had been the first to move, opposes the other. He strikes him in the body—it is a fearful blow, as if a great tree had bent its top to the ground, and then sprang straight again—and the tall one, broken in the middle, falls back into the swamp. And now, on both sides, all the rocks and boulders are moving, the sleepers are waking, and I on the causeway can no more endure it. I faint, I die. I think it is death . . ."

Mr Byculla was deeply moved by the recollection of his dream, but in a little while, after Lessing had asked a few questions, he recovered his usual composure and even showed something of the ebullience that often distinguished him. He was, it appeared, a little vain of his capacity to dream with so fearful an imagination.

Lessing had wanted him, when he arrived, to relax in the usual way and tap, if he could, the wells of memory; but Mr Byculla had insisted on first relating the newest coinage of the night. Now complaisant, he lay down and tried to let his words flow free and innocent from the uncensored depths of his mind; but either he did not try hard enough or memory was quite occluded by present circumstance. He had very little to say, and that little came haltingly and was manifestly dressed for the occasion.—Mr Byculla, indeed, was the first to suggest that they were wasting time, and for that day, at any rate, the pretence of treatment had better be abandoned. "I am not in the mood," he explained, with a gesture of apology.

Lessing made tentative reference to a drug that he had sometimes used with success, but Mr Byculla would have nothing to do with it.

"It might save time," said Lessing.

"That is a subject to which I have been giving some close attention in the last few days," said Mr Byculla. "The subject of time.—I am but a bird of passage, Dr Lessing. I am here to-day, and gone, perhaps, the week after next. I am most restless man. And I have been asking myself this question: if I must go away before my treatment is finished, before you have cured me, will I suffer any ill-effects from premature breaking-off of our association?"

"I don't think I could guarantee to 'cure' you, as you put it, however long I might treat you. I would try to help you, with some confidence, I may say, to rationalise your dreams——"

"They are terrible, are they not?"

"—but apart from them, and the temporary, though recurrent, distress they seem to cause you, you're not suffering from any very obvious neurotic disturbance——"

"No, no, I am most healthy man. I have good appetite, good digestion."

"—and I could let you go, at any time, without anxiety about your general condition. So far, I'm afraid, I've done nothing at all for you——"

"But you have! You have indeed. No one but

150

you, no one since my father died, has ever listened patiently to my dreams, though I have often wanted to speak of them. And you are much better, more sympathetic, than my father; for he listened to me only on condition that I would thereafter listen to his beastly dreams, which he thought were most wonderful, though in fact they were dull as ditch-water."

"I have no intention of telling you mine," said Lessing, "however long we may continue the treatment. I hope we shall continue it, if your restlessness isn't too much for you, but if you're determined not to behave like a patient to-day, I'm not going to try and persuade you. Let us go next door and have a drink instead. I have to go out in half an hour or so, but we've time for a glass of sherry."

"I shall be delighted," said Mr Byculla, and they went into the sitting-room, where they found Claire, in a domestic mood, knitting a jersey for the child. For the last day or two she had been gentle of voice, affectionately careful of her daughter and of Lessing so far as he would permit it, and conspicuously devoted to household tasks. She was very pleased to drink a glass of sherry with them, and seemed genuinely disappointed when, after some forty minutes, Lessing said he must go.

"But don't let me take you away," he said to Mr Byculla. "Stay and have another drink with Claire; I'm sure she'd like you to."

"Of course I would," said Claire, "but I wish you hadn't got to go, George. I knew you were going out to dinner, but I had no idea you would be in such a hurry."

"It's not a party I'm going to. Harrow asked me to look at a patient of his, at the Royal Northern, and have a quick meal with him afterwards to talk about the case. That's all."

"So you'll be back quite early?"

"Yes, but not as early as I'd expected. Your cousin Ronnie rang me up at the clinic this morning——"

"What did he say?"

"He asked me to look in and see him some time to-day. He's got something on his mind, I don't know what——"

"You're not going, are you?"

"Yes, I said I would. He's no friend of mine, but apparently he needs someone to take an interest in him. I said I couldn't come much before nine——"

"You're going to his flat?"

"Yes, though he's not living there now, he told me. He telephoned from Brighton, and said he'd come up for the day and go back by the last train."

"He'll only try to borrow money from you."

"I think money isn't his worst trouble at the moment."

"Don't go, George!"

"Of course I'm going. I said I would. But I shan't be late.—When shall we see you again, Mr Byculla? Before next Tuesday?"

"Leave it to me," said Mr Byculla. "I will make some good arrangement."

"Good night, then."

Claire stood by the fireplace with a tense and haggard look on her face, her eyes astare; and her voice trembled when she spoke. "He mustn't go!" she said. "He mustn't see Ronnie!"

"Is it for your husband you are concerned, or for Ronnie?" asked Mr Byculla.

"For George."

"This meeting will make him unhappy?"

"It's worse than that."

She took up the telephone, and with nervous finger dialled a number. She listened anxiously, but there was no reply.

"He isn't in," she said, "and I don't know where to find him. Oh, what can I do?"

"Your husband," said Mr Byculla, "observed in parenthesis that Ronnie was no friend of his. But he is, perhaps, a friend of yours?"

"He was."

"Not now?"

"I hope I'll never see him again."

There was silence for a little while, and then Mr Byculla said, "I am not, alas, sufficiently old friend of the family to make intimate enquiry in this matter, but if I could help you in any way——"

"I don't see how you can."

In a gentle voice, like a dentist soothing a nervous patient, Mr Byculla asked, "Why does this young man Ronnie so urgently desire to speak to your good husband?''

"He's got an idea—it's the damnedest idiocy—that his father may have murdered a girl——''

"The late Sir Simon? Oh, no! That is impossible.''

"Of course it is. But Ronnie found a five-pound note . . .''

With exasperation, in disjointed phrases, she told the whole story, and Mr Byculla, listening with courteous attention, disentangled her narrative with patience and discretion, with no evidence of surprise except when she told him that the dead girl's five pounds had been given her by Ronnie Killaloe. "It is a small world, Mrs Lessing!'' he observed with the air of one who makes a profound discovery.

"So you see,'' she concluded, "that even if I'd told him it was George who sent his father the note, it wouldn't have done any good. He'd just have wanted to know where George got it.—And you do see, don't you, that they *mustn't* meet? I told George a lie about the note, not for my own sake, not really, but so as not to make him unhappy; for Ronnie would let the cat out of the bag right away.''

"You do not know from whom Dr Lessing did obtain the note?''

"I didn't like to ask him. We'd had a quarrel about it, and got over that—or it simmered down—and to ask questions would have started him off again. And that was the last thing I wanted.''

His legs crossed and his right knee clasped in his folded hands, Mr Byculla in a deep chair wore a look of comfortable benignity, and Claire was much calmer now. He had given her confidence, and confidence had become an almost childish faith in his ability to save her from the disaster that threatened. He had accepted responsibility, and she, acquiescent and almost content, had now only to wait for his decision.—She waited, without impatience, a little fascinated by the stillness of his long body, the composure of his heavy features. His unusually large finger-nails, polished and conspicuous on his clasped hands, reminded her, incongruously, of a pony that for several years had been the delight of her childhood. It would wrinkle back its lips, as though grinning its welcome, and show great yellow-ish teeth when she brought it sugar. She had taught it to raise its mouth for a kiss . . .

"If you were to inform Ronnie that you had been told, by your husband, who gave him this five-pound note, that would demolish all reason for their meeting," said Mr Byculla after a long silence.

"But he won't tell me, if I don't ask him, and I've no intention of asking. He probably doesn't remember, in any case."

"He remembered the number of the note."

"That's the sort of thing he does notice. Small silly things of no importance. But he's terribly forgetful otherwise."

"It was, perhaps, one of his patients who gave it him. Perhaps I was that patient."

155

"But you weren't, were you?—Oh, of course you weren't!"

Mr Byculla, smiling, gently shook his head. "It would, however, be helpful to tell Ronnie so," he said. "There is no reason why he should not believe you."

"Just to prevent him talking to George?"

"That is what you want to prevent."

"But then he'd come and see you. He'd make a nuisance of himself."

"I may not stay in London much longer. I was telling your husband this afternoon that I am most restless man, a mere bird of passage. When Ronnie comes to see me, perhaps I will have hopped from the twig.—Telephone again, to see if he is in."

Again there was no reply, and Mr Byculla asked, "Does he live far from here?"

She told him Ronnie's address, and Mr Byculla, looking at his watch, declared, "There is plenty of time. He will be in before long, no doubt, and you will tell him to alter his plans. He must not wait for your husband, you will say, because there is no longer any reason for them to meet. You have discovered, you will then inform him, that it was your husband who sent this note of ill omen to the late Sir Simon, and you know from whom Dr Lessing procured it. You will ask Ronnie to take you out to dinner, and at dinner, you say, you will tell him all. —Will that not persuade him to break his engagement?"

"I think it would. In fact, I'm sure it would. But what will George do, if he goes to Ronnie's flat and finds no one there?"

"The normal course of action for a disappointed visitor is to wait a little while, and then go home."

"In a bad temper," said Claire. "And if, when he comes home, he finds that his wife has gone out, his temper will get worse and worse."

"You can leave a short letter for him, by which to explain your absence. You should say something like this: '*Ronnie only wanted to borrow money from you——*'"

"That's what I told him!"

"It is always a highly probable motive.—'*Ronnie only wanted to borrow money, and I was determined that he should not worry you. Therefore I have persuaded him to come out with me, and I will use all my influence to prevent him from pestering you in future.*'—Write something like that."

"George will be angry with me for going out with Ronnie."

"But you must, in order to prevent his meeting with Dr Lessing; and also you must find some good excuse for going.—Well, what is better, I say, than the honest plea of connubial devotion?"

"I suppose you're right," said Claire, but went with some reluctance to her desk and in manifest discomfort composed her letter. She showed it to Mr Byculla, who approved of it, and said, "Now telephone once more, and see if he is in."

"Yes," she whispered, a minute later, her hand over the mouthpiece. "He's there!"

"You know what to say," said Mr Byculla, and listened complacently to the conversation that ensued.

CHAPTER SIXTEEN

WITHOUT much difficulty Mr Byculla found his way to the house in Batavia Street, off Warwick Avenue, where Ronnie had an attic-flat, and through the outer door, that stood open, walked upstairs. Just above the second landing he trod on a loose board that cracked like a breaking stick.

He knocked softly at Ronnie's door, waited for half a minute, and examined the lock. The door was loose on its hinges, the lock was old. He picked it easily, with something of contempt, indeed, for so trivial an obstacle; and turned on the light. He looked at his watch and saw that it was twenty minutes to nine.

The shabby rooms with their dilapidated furniture offended his eyes, and displeased his nose a little. He showed no interest in Ronnie's possessions, but from a small table removed a framed photograph of Claire in uniform, and put it into a drawer. He sat down in a creaking chair to wait for Lessing, and seven or eight minutes later heard footsteps on the stair; and the loose board cracked loudly. He got up, and with a propitiatory smile on his face opened the door.

"You were going to ask me what the devil I am doing here," he said cheerfully, before Lessing, his tongue bitted by surprise, could speak. "Well, come inside and I will tell you, Doctor. I have a good explanation."

"I certainly didn't expect to find you here," said Lessing. "Has anything happened?"

"No, no. You must not be worried."

"Is young Killaloe here?"

"No.—But sit down, and I will tell you."

With a distaste as manifest as Mr Byculla's, Lessing looked round the dreary room and asked, "Have you been here before?"

"Never. It was your wife who told me the address. She is with her cousin now."

"Claire—and Killaloe? You mean——?"

"You must not be upset. It is for your sake she has gone out with him. She did not want him to meet you."

"Why not?"

"She was afraid," said Mr Byculla with a sigh—in a voice that seemed to deprecate and deny the suggestion even as he uttered it—"She was afraid he might do you an injury."

"What utter nonsense! Why should he?"

The delicacy of Mr Byculla's manner was such that even Lessing could not be offended by his reply: "It appears that he is somewhat in love with your wife."

"He may be; but he's not the sort to make that an excuse for quarrelling with me."

"Your wife thinks otherwise. She told me about a most curious coincidence in his life; which, as we

160

know, has been not at all the sort of life one would expect of a son of the late Sir Simon. No, indeed! But I had not supposed he was of violent disposition until Mrs Lessing drew my attention to the fact, so obvious but hitherto not observed by the public, that the unfortunate young woman called Fanny Bruce and his father, the late Sir Simon, both came to their untimely end in precisely the same fashion. By reason, that is to say, of a broken neck.''

''But there's nothing in that! His father's death was accidental, there was never a suggestion of anything else, and as to the girl—well, Ronnie was found not guilty.''

''It seems, however, that Mrs Lessing has been much concerned about the coincidence. and when she heard that her cousin, who is no longer living in this flat, had asked you to meet him here, she became highly nervous and greatly worried.''

''It's a ridiculous assumption,'' said Lessing, but looked about him, at Ronnie's shabby furniture, with a new and disquieted interest.

''I think so also,'' said Mr Byculla cheerfully. ''But if—for sake of argument only, of course—if one pretends the assumption is not so wild, and if, to-morrow morning or the next day, there was a lamentable discovery here, of another victim with his neck broken, the coincidence would be greatly reinforced and obvious to all beholders.''

''Ronnie, in that case, would be in a very awkward position—but as the original assumption is wholly fictitious, the final catastrophe isn't likely to occur.''

"Nevertheless, it was that fearful picture which Mrs Lessing had in mind."

"She must be going off her head," said Lessing irritably. "Ronnie had nothing to do with his father's death, and he's certainly not man enough to try and murder me."

"You were not uneasy about meeting him here?"

"Of course not."

"You are not a timorous man, Doctor?"

"I make no pretence to bravery, but I've got a certain amount of common sense. The owner of a room like this couldn't inspire fear in any one."

Lessing got up and looked impatiently at a lithograph, framed in *passe-partout*, that hung upon a peeling wall. Dust lay thickly on the glass. He took, with distaste, a book from a scantily furnished shelf, and shrugged his shoulders, and dropped it on a table.

"To have common sense," said Mr Byculla softly, "is more rare than being brave. If we all had good sense, there are many things that frighten us now to which we should pay no attention. Death itself. Death should never frighten a man of sense. It is not a strange thing, death. It is a part of life, like birth. One cries a little, but there is no need to be afraid . . ."

Mr Byculla, relaxed and easy, was talking to himself, as it seemed, for his voice was gentle and made on demand on Lessing's attention. Nor did Lessing pay attention, for in his idle, irritable survey of the

162

room he had pulled open a drawer and found a framed photograph of Claire in uniform.

Abruptly he asked, "Did Claire say anything about her relations with Ronnie?"

"She told me he was in love with her. It worried her, I think."

"Anything about her feelings towards him?"

"No, no. I am not so old a friend that she could talk with intimacy on such a topic."

"Did she say anything about a five-pound note?"

Mr Byculla did not immediately reply, and Lessing again demanded, "Did she?"

"Yes," said Mr Byculla, "she told me about it."

"You gave it to me, and I sent it to Sir Simon. Then I found it in her handbag.—Was it Ronnie who gave it to her?"

"That is what she said."

In the glare of the light that hung close above his head the little muscles at the corner of Lessing's mouth bubbled and leapt like water boiling in a pot. With agitated fingers he felt for his pocket-book, and taking from it the twice-folded note, spread it open, under the light, and stared at it as if by concentration he could read upon it the whole story of his betrayal.

Mr Byculla rose quietly, and from behind him looked over his shoulder.

"Yes," he said sadly, "that is it. *Mujhe afsos hai, Sahib, lekin ab ap sidhe raste men hain.*"—And anyone listening might have heard a sharp and sudden noise,

163

as if another visitor had stepped heavily on the loose stair-board; or as if a stick had been broken.

A minute or two later Mr Byculla came out of the house, alone, and with the key he had procured unlocked the door of Lessing's motor-car, that stood at the pavement edge. Swiftly, but not recklessly, he drove eastward, and halting in Northumberland Avenue, unobtrusively abandoned the borrowed car, and walked to the Charing Cross Hotel.

CHAPTER SEVENTEEN

FOR no reason that was apparent at the time, Mr Byculla had registered at the Charing Cross Hotel as M. André Boileau, of Lyons, and in his bedroom, to fortify him in his new character and remind him of it, were several Paris newspapers and an anthology of French poetry. The book lay open on his dressing-table, and above it the looking-glass now reflected a visage of dire melancholy and eyes that were red with weeping. For a minute or more he looked sadly at the image of his grief, and then, glancing at the printed page, was more deeply moved—but none the less, a little pleased—to see how appropriate were the verses:

> " *Mais, vrai, j'ai trop pleuré. Les aubes sont navrantes,*
> *Toute lune est atroce et tout soleil amer . . .* "

He read them aloud, in a choking voice, and for comfort opened the shipmaster's case of bottles and glasses that he had bought for Sir Simon's comfort. There was a little brandy left, and drinking half of what was there, he took up the telephone and asked a clerk at the Reception Desk to make his bill ready, for he was leaving at once.

From the lining of his old-fashioned Gladstone bag he took the three passports that he found it convenient to carry, and returning two to their hiding-place, put in his coat-pocket that issued by the French Republic. He packed quickly, like a man accustomed to it, and within three or four minutes was downstairs, his luggage beside him, and paying his bill. He spoke with a French accent, a trilling in the throat, and was presently in a taxi-cab on his way to Victoria.

He arrived there at seventeen minutes to ten, and the porter who took his luggage guided him to the proper ticket-office.

"*Un billet, Marseille, deuxième classe,*" said Mr Byculla, and pretended to have some difficulty in understanding how much he was asked to pay.

"Eight pounds, four shillings, and four," he said, slowly and thickly, and fumbled with his money. Among the notes that he took from his wallet was one, much folded, that he opened and laid flat with slow, reluctant fingers; and before he passed it through the *guichet* there fell on it two water-drops, two heavy tears.

His porter, a little contemptuous of continental emotion, but protectively sorry for the foreign gentleman's grief, led him quickly to the platform where the night boat-train to France was waiting, and found him a seat. Mr Byculla, tipping hand-somely, looked about him at his fellow-passengers, and almost at once was interested in a group of four that stood beside the coach in which he was to travel.

Most conspicuous of them was a tall and hand-

166

some woman, a little past her youth, whose cheeks were straitened by grief and whose voice rang high with wrath. Her companions were a pretty, hatless girl with red hair, a slim dark youth with the carriage of a dancer, and another man, short and squat, of frog-like countenance, who, perhaps because of the fur collar on his coat, looked as though he might have some connexion with the theatre.

Walking slowly past them, Mr Byculla heard enough of their conversation, which was in French, to conclude that all of them made their living on or near the stage. He looked back, over his shoulder, at the tall woman whose sorrow shone like pearls upon her cheek, and with poetry fresh in his mind murmured to himself:

> " *Qu'as-tu fait, ô toi que voilà*
> *Pleurant sans cesse,*
> *Dis, qu'as-tu fait, toi que voilà,*
> *De ta jeunesse?* "

He turned, and loitering deliberately, passed them again.—There had been a quarrel, she was complaining bitterly of injustice. Her contract had been ignored, it was formidable and altogether beyond belief that she should be required to return to Paris when her contract had quite clearly guaranteed her an engagement of eight weeks, with nothing at all said about personal behaviour.—The red-haired girl and the young man who looked like a dancer sympathised with her loudly, but the older man, with a fur collar to his coat, shrugged his shoulders and said one must take the rough with the smooth.

A whistle blew, doors were slammed, and Mr Byculla boarded the train. The tall and handsome woman followed him, but stood by the window at the end of the coach until the train began to move. Her companions cried good-bye, called their good wishes, and she, leaning out, made an effort to seem unafraid and capable of matching her spirit to disappointment.

"*Ce n'est pas gaie, la vie d'artiste!*" she shouted brazenly.

She found her seat, took off her hat, and with a little handkerchief of lace and frills dabbed at her runnelled cheeks. Then, raising her head, looked up to see who was her neighbour; and on the opposite seat saw Mr Byculla regarding her with sad, and sympathetic, and speculative eyes.